TRICKSTER TALES

TRICKSTER TALES

Leanbh Pearson

Trickster Tales

Edited by: Candace Nola

Formatted by: Stephanie Ellis

Cover illustration by: Greg Chapman

First Edition: November 2025

ISBN (paperback): 978-1-963355-41-3

ISBN (ebook): 978-1-963355-40-6

Library of Congress Control Number:

BRIGIDS GATE PRESS
Overland Park, Kansas
www.brigidsgatepress.com

*"To Tracey.
My companion in all things wild, weird and mischievous. This one's for you."*

"Ginnungagap which looked toward the north parts was filled with thick and heavy ice and rime, and everywhere within were fogs and gusts; but the south side of Ginnungagap was lightened by the sparks and gledes that flew out of Muspellheim."

'Gylfi's Mocking'
The Prose Edda by Snorri Sturluson
Translated by Sir George Webbe Dasent, 1842

Contents

The Beginning

Odin stared hard at Loki, his single cobalt blue eye assessing. Despite Odin sacrificing the one eye for wisdom in a time when the Nine Worlds were still young, Loki still found the *knowing* behind the brightness of that gaze unnerving. The All-Father was calculating and planning something. Loki was a Trickster and he, above all beings, knew the look of someone scheming when he saw it. Whatever Odin was planning unnerved him. This was too crucial a meeting between warring gods for any plans that might jeopardise a peaceful outcome.

"You want to *what?*" Loki asked.

Odin cast a sidelong glance at the envoy party standing nearby. "I don't trust them."

The Vanir had assembled themselves in a tight, defensive cluster at the centre of Odin's Hall of Valhalla. Although it was a small envoy, the host of gods and goddesses present was the most significant among their race. These were the gods Odin had tried to crush beneath Thor's brute strength, outmanoeuvre with Tyr's skilful swordsmanship, and defeat with his own tactical cunning. But the Vanir persisted, neither bending nor breaking, and all without a true king among them. Njord, ruler of the ocean depths, was the oldest surviving god. He was also the father of many of the Vanir present. But to Odin's surprise, they seemed to be ruled by an older woman: a witch. She was neither intimidated nor frightened by Odin and his host of warriors. Despite the shield-walls of bristling steel and flying arrows, the Vanir witch remained unbending before Odin and the Aesir.

Worse for Odin, the Vanir held sway over the mortal men and women of Midgard, and prayers were offered to the Vanir with a regular devotion that was unparalleled. Naturally, Odin saw this inequality of worship as bartering pieces he might use to win the war by assimilating the Vanir into the Aesir. But Loki, Trickster and schemer, knew no matter how many times mortals of Midgard prayed to warrior-deities like Odin, Thor, and Tyr, when drought or famine threatened, when seeking bountiful harvests or full fishing nets, mortals would pray to the Vanir.

"*You* don't trust *them*?" Loki asked, incredulous.

He looked purposefully from Odin to the Vanir. The situation reminded him uncomfortably of how Odin spoke of the giants and, by extension, himself. Odin knew the power that the Vanir possessed was independent of him and he hated anything beyond his control.

Odin leaned closer, speaking conspiratorially. "There's great power among them, Loki. A power we could use. The witch who leads them is skilled in *seidr*, and she won't offer it to me willingly. She won't even teach it to me. Until we bring the Vanir to heel, she'll always be a threat to me."

"You plan to destroy them, then?"

"What else would you have me do with such vipers in our nest?"

Loki gaped. He must be mistaken. "What you're suggesting is to break the Guest-Laws of protection and peace. That's the worst trickery imaginable and it won't solve this situation. What you're suggesting will only lead to Vanir and Aesir bloodshed in your own hall."

"Which is why I seek advice from one more skilled than me in trickery and falsehood. Are you not he, aren't you the Loki I first met when the Nine Worlds were created?"

"The same thing you accuse the Vanir of being, you use against the giants, against my kinsfolk and, thereby, accuse me."

"You heard Gullveig speak only moments ago. The wisdom of eons falls from her lips. Think how much knowledge she can access and think of the benefit the gift of prophecy would offer us if she shared it with me."

"She'll never share it willingly with you. She's a leader of the Vanir and just as cunning as you. What you want will lead us all into greater bloodshed than you propose tonight. Do you need me to repeat that a third time? Have you heard my warning now?"

"Knowledge is necessary for our survival, Loki. If I possessed *seidr*, I might avoid bloodshed at every turn."

Loki laughed bitterly. "If Gullveig grants this gift to you, would you prevent bloodshed for those in Jotunheim too? The giants have always been your enemies. Or would knowing the future only be used for you to benefit the Aesir?"

"The Aesir must survive above all else, brother."

Loki crossed his arms over his chest. "Of course. I understand that. I know who you are, *brother*. But I'll have no part in this action. Convince Gullveig to share seidr with you if you can. If you cannot, I'll not be part of killing a guest in Valhalla.

Loki wanted nothing more than to be anywhere else right now. Both he and Odin had made a pledge as brothers and its bond tied them more closely than many brothers who shared blood. Loki still remembered how attractive the gift and its potential Odin had offered him. To be free from Muspellheim and his malformed body was a promise of power.

Odin had taken Loki when he was a misshapen, misbegotten giant from Muspellheim. He'd transformed his body into one that was elegant, handsome like the Aesir, lithe and enigmatic. And in gratitude, Loki had bound himself in kinship to Odin. He'd follow wherever Odin led, even when he waged war against the frost giants of Jotunheim. But now Odin was proposing to take sword and axe to this witch in his own hall, shedding blood under the truce of Guest-Law.

"Where Gullveig is resolute, her apprentice, Freyja, looks ambitious. I might persuade her, don't you think?"

Loki let his gaze run appreciably over Freyja, stopping at the sheathed long sword. "She looks like a shield-maiden."

"Such warriors are valuable. I've already consulted with Mimir's head."

"I don't care what counsel Mimir gave you, I want no part in this."

"I need only your presence beside me, brother. Gullveig will suspect nothing if you remain beside me. Remember, *seidr* is the only way to protect the Nine Worlds."

Loki swallowed the honeyed mead in one gulp, but it tasted bitter. "Odin, please reconsider. This isn't wise."

"Have you the gift of prophecy now, Loki? Many of your ideas aren't wise and I've never grumbled."

"What makes you certain Freyja even knows *seidr*? What if you destroy Gullveig and lose *seidr* forever?"

"See how Freyja clings to Gullveig's side? She is her closest confidant, a true apprentice and ally. I'll use whatever tactics I need to win this war."

Loki refilled his cup, drinking heavily. "You'll regret this moment."

At the end of the hall, the Aesir and Vanir had broken their uneasy standoff and now mingled, eating and drinking with each other as they walked along the long tables laden with the bountiful feast. In this moment, there seemed little inclination to fight. *Perhaps Odin is right? Perhaps without Gullveig, these two races can unite peacefully?*

Loki's gaze flicked to Gullveig, the witch standing tall and proud, her dark hair streaked with silver. She *was* like a boulder in a river current; the water passing around her, separating the stream she stood within, resilient and unmoving. Loki lounged in his engraved chair beside Odin and Frigg's more elaborate ones. He watched Gullveig's eyes follow Odin around the hall, never straying from him. Beside Gullveig, Freyja was motionless. She was tall, blonde hair artfully braided, her comely form clothed in the shimmer of chain mail. Loki focused on the long, bone-handled blade she wore at her hip. The sword looked comfortable on her. While Loki studied her thoughtfully, her piercing blue eyes fixed on him.

Loki raised his goblet with a feigned drunken gesture and tipped it back, swallowing more of the honeyed mead. It curdled in his stomach. He wasn't certain Odin was right about Freyja. She was undoubtedly the most beautiful among the Vanir, known for stirring men's hearts to passion: to love and war, both. But to Loki, Freyja seemed no more amenable than the witch Gullveig. Of course, Odin would never know how Freyja might react until they removed Gullveig from her side. He slouched in his chair and wished himself anywhere else. He scowled into the hearth flames, barely stirring when Odin sat in the chair beside him. Then, with a gesture, Odin brought the attention of everyone in Valhalla to him.

Odin smiled like a hunter luring prey to slaughter. "Gullveig, I'm much impressed by the art of *seidr*. Come, teach it to me. Show me once more?"

Loki stared more intently at the flames. He heard the whisper of movement across the floor as Gullveig stepped forward to Odin. Loki held his breath and willed another course of action, another series of events, to play out this night. From where he sat, he saw Gullveig shake her head in refusal again. The tension filled Valhalla.

Odin stood, his ravens dislodged from his shoulders in a flurry of feathers, and flames erupted around Gullveig.

Unable to flee, Loki cringed in his chair, the witch screaming as she burned. He'd imagined the many alternate paths to peace which Odin had cast aside in pride and arrogance. The unendurable burning continued, and Loki drank more mead until he no longer tasted it. He kept his eyes on Freyja as she stared in horror and outrage while Gullveig burned a second and third time. Her flesh regenerated, burning and healing anew as the flames continued. Loki wasn't sure he could remain seated, but, fixed by horror, he couldn't force his limbs to move either. Gullveig began to speak, her lips a burnt ruin, her throat scorched and raw. But the power of the völva was unparalleled and in her thrice-burned flesh, she gave Odin one final lesson in seidr:

"The Nine Worlds lashed by the greatest of winters,
Brother will fight brother, kin will slay kin,
In the age of axes, swords, shields, and wolves,
Ravenous Fenrir will break his bonds,
And so the twilight of the Nine Words begins."

There was a *thwack* of a spear hitting flesh and splintering bone. Then, a final scream that echoed eerily. Finally, death took Gullveig in smouldering flames and burning flesh.

Loki huddled in his chair. He was chilled despite the blazing fire in the hearth. Gullveig's final words of prophecy ran like ice in his veins.

THE TRAITOR'S CURSE

Loki was dying on the shores of Helheim. There seemed little point denying it. *What made me remember Gullveig all these eons later?* The ashen shores beneath him were frigid, and icy waves lapped at his thighs. In time, the water would cover his chest. And, when it reached his mouth, he would drown. Despite his hopeless predicament, Loki still wanted to survive. Motionless on his back in the shallow water, he stared at the sky, now as black as Surt, embers raining down from the burning branches of Yggdrasil as the Nine Worlds imploded. *This bountiful chaos is my creation. Well, Odin's and mine. Together, we made Ragnarök as glorious and terrible as Gullveig prophesied. I might as well enjoy it to its very end.*

Around him were the scattered corpses of the gods: Vanir and Aesir alike mingled with the bodies of giants and elves. There was no divide in death—the golden gods of Asgard had fallen beside Jotunheim's frost-rimed giants just as easily as Muspellheim's meteorite-clad warriors had succumbed. Battle spared none, and even the Valkyries, the shadowy shield-maidens on their ghostly mounts, were among the fallen. Ragnarök: the fateful battle where they'd all died, and now the Nine Worlds were sinking into the waves of Niflheim before Yggdrasil would sprout again. Or so Gullveig had prophesied. Loki couldn't help but wonder if she'd even told the truth. That cunning witch could have lied to them all, promised rebirth when there was none. *Wouldn't that be a fine jest? All of us dying and taking the Nine Worlds with us for our pride, arrogance, and vengeance.*

A frigid realization sank into him. One goddess had been absent on the battlefield. The Valkyries had fought like vengeful shield-maidens, but where was their leader? In the turmoil of battle, Loki hadn't once seen Freyja in her chain mail. The combat between Loki's two sons and their enemies; Odin and Fenrir, the monstrous wolf, devouring Odin, Thor and the serpent Jörmungand falling together. Heimdall had engaged Loki in combat, and he'd only seen glimpses of Freyja's brother, the golden swordsman Freyr challenging Surt, the Lord of Muspellheim. And with Heimdall dead beside him, Loki mortally wounded, he'd watched the duel between Freyr and Surt as Yggdrasil burned above them.

Ragnarök was the prophecy Gullveig had delivered to Odin that night in Valhalla when he killed her. Now, the Nine Worlds were soaked in blood, and from those grim seeds, nurtured with the bitter salt waters of Niflheim and fed by the fiery rain from Yggdrasil's burning, Loki dared not imagine what future might grow from the fertile battlefield.

Loki turned his head to regard Odin, once his brother and enemy, now a broken body on the bloody ground. The enormous wolf, Fenrir, Loki's son, was finally still. He'd torn Odin into pieces before falling, his massive snout a hideous ruin, the lower jaw torn free. Loki's other son, Jörmungand, washed up on the shore, Thor's body only nine steps away. All Loki's children with the witch Angrboda had been the instruments of Odin's downfall. Loki had tried to warn him that his arrogance would be his undoing, but Odin refused to listen. *But you tried to break me beneath your will, Odin. Ragnarök was exactly what you deserved, brother.*

Blood frothed on Loki's lips, and sudden pain blossomed through his chest. The cold ocean water carried him on its tide, sending shivers of fresh pain. He struggled to breathe, lungs pushing against the broken sternum, fractured ribs forced to take the strain of his weight. He convulsed with agony, pulled under the water by the current, weakly struggling to the surface again. Loki broke above the dark water and wheezed, bloody spittle running down his chin.

A thick white mist hung above the frosted sands and wisps curled upward to form three white-robed figures. Loki cursed again, recognizing them before they had even fully materialized. He held his breath as they stepped forward from the mist, barefoot on the icy sands. The Norns were as familiar with death as the Valkyries, but these three women were not battle-maidens in service to Freyja. These were the three most powerful witches in the Nine Worlds. *And they choose to visit me now. Why?*

"Still alive, then?" a cold voice asked.

Where were the Norns? Above him, Yggdrasil was a blazing inferno, embers blowing across the starless sky, but he could see no one else. *Did*

I imagine the voice? An icy wind blew across the barren shores, churning the frozen waters, washing against him again. He hissed in agony, salt water soaking into his chest wound, the tide dragging at him. The waves lifted him once more, slapping him against the shore. He screamed, the chest wound tearing at its ragged edges, and cursed every god, every Midgard whoreson who ever held a sword, the dwarf metalsmiths, and Odin for his foolish pride.

"Those are some inventive curses, Loki."

He jerked at the familiar voice, trying to breathe slowly through the agony of the axe-wound in his chest. He stared up at Freyja.

"You cowardly bitch."

She laughed, seductive as honey and sharp as knives. "You should've known better than to taunt those with power over you."

"What do you want? I don't think we have much time left for conversation."

She put a long finger to her cheek and pouted as if thinking. "I want the Nine Worlds as they were before Odin and his Aesir took them from us. I want you gone. You know what I'm speaking about, don't you, clever Loki?"

Loki nodded, forcing himself to float as another wave tossed him on the tide. He screamed again, more curses pouring from his lips, and coughed, blood on his lips and in the surrounding water.

"Loki?"

"What?"

"You always were trouble," she said, perfumed scent hanging in the air.

Cold steel touched his throat. He opened his eyes, not realizing he'd closed them. Weakly, he flailed in the water, staring at the sword tip Freyja pressed to his skin. That sword, which was always sheathed across her back, the shining extension of her vengeance. *What is she doing? Why slit my throat when I'm already dying?*

"Freyja," he began.

She shook her head, expression one of mock sorrow. Loki moved his lips to speak, demand answers. But there was no sound. Only gurgling blood spilled from his lips, pouring into the ocean. *In the Nine Worlds, why?* He slapped his arms uselessly against the waves and he watched the hem of Freyja's tunic and her chain mail stain with his blood. The ocean swell was rising quickly, and the red tide was already above Freyja's mid-thigh. *Why has she done this?*

Loki struggled to breathe, blood pooling around his collarbones. His lungs worked like bellows, but blood only sucked back into the axe-wound at his chest with every breath. He stared at Freyja, pale and magnificent in her armour, unblemished by battle and blood. *She never even ventured into battle.* She returned his gaze without pity, eyes as cold as the scarlet hoarfrost on his armour.

"Without you, the Nine Worlds will be as Gullveig intended."

Loki's mouth opened, lips moving wordlessly. *This is about vengeance? All this has been about vengeance?* Freyja pushed him out into the swell of the waves, lifeblood seeping further into the water. The darkness, oblivion, and re-beginning of Ginnungagap waited for him. Without *you* in the Nine Worlds? He considered her final words as darkness engulfed him. *Does she intend to prevent my return when Yggdrasil grows anew?* But he was dying and would find out the answer soon enough.

THE VOID

The darkness of the void rushed him, tugging at the fabric of his being, tearing away shreds of memory even before his body had sunk below Niflheim's waters. Loki's failing heartbeat grew weaker, evanescence only moments away. Ginnungagap: the void that separates flesh from shade. It cleaved him apart as easily as a blade slicing skin from muscle. He was one of the most ancient beings of the Nine Worlds, but he heard Freyja's haunting chant, her curse echoing as she banished him, forbidding his shade to reunite with his flesh, and casting him forever into the vast emptiness of the void.

Caught adrift, disembodied, and unencumbered by physical constraint, Loki stared at Yggdrasil. The World Tree had appeared mighty throughout his existence, but now it was just a burnt skeleton of bare branches, icy waters of Niflheim lapping around its exposed roots. Flames still spread along its upper branches, and there was a tremendous crack as the trunk splintered apart. The roots flared white-hot with intense heat as the horrid white Nidhöggr devoured the last of its central roots. Nidhöggr broke free from his prison, unfurling pale wings to rise into the starless expanse of the dead sky. Fenrir's brothers, the wolves Sköll and Hati, had consumed the heavens while the battle had raged.

Loki drifted further from the broken remnants of the Nine Worlds, watching Yggdrasil fall into the ocean. The Nine Worlds were extinguished in a wave of kinetic energy that swept across Ginnungagap, blowing Loki further from the cosmos he had known. Spinning, twisting through the darkness, Loki saw steam rising from the ocean, a sapling sprouting and leaves unfurling with tiny stars already blossoming along its branches. Yggdrasil rose anew, the small pinpricks of starlight growing larger and brighter until Yggdrasil stood tall with the Nine Worlds glittering anew among its branches. The pale dragon Nidhöggr circled Jotunheim, disappearing into the northern mountains to await the next Ragnarök. But Loki wouldn't see it. He fought against Freyja's curse, but it pushed him further from the Nine Worlds.

Time and space unravelled behind him like threads falling from the Norn's loom. Had those three witches who wove the fates for all in the Nine Worlds allowed Freyja to weave another? Or had it been unseen? The Norns had come to him on the shore just before Freyja appeared. Had they intended to warn him? Loki didn't know. And now, lost to the darkness, the question was pointless.

A distant constellation in the darkness shone brightly. His bindings to the Nine Worlds like gossamer strands, the unfamiliar stars pulled like a loadstone. There was something else there, an awareness brushing at his frayed edges. Stardust of an ancient constellation surrounded Loki and something else—a foreign consciousness assessing him.

"Trickster," the being whispered.

Hands of stardust gently held Loki above another swirling cosmos. This world, unlike his own, a constellation with a single pale blue globe like an eggshell at its centre, a speckled trail of stardust encircling it. Within the centre of that pale blue light was a swirling heart of red flame, twisting colours of the globe like two entwined serpents.

The brush of the greater awareness against his own was enough to make Loki feel small again. Yet where Freyja had tried to defeat him, he refused to succumb to the primordial darkness of Ginnungagap. The ancient being who had summoned him across the liminal space breathed new life into his form. Full of determination and fire, Loki plummeted to the pale eggshell of a planet below him.

Transformation

Loki opened his eyes to a twisting column of orange flame against a vibrant blue sky. *Muspellheim never had such blue skies.* He pushed upright into a sitting position. There was soft sand beneath his palms. *White sand at that.* Muspelheim was all basalt shards or volcanic glass fit to shred skin. There was nothing so kind as sand there. Awareness of his surroundings brought new realizations. He was naked without a shred of clothing and, second, this body was female. *What in the Nine Worlds has happened to me?*

Loki's new body was young, long-limbed, and lithe. Oh, Loki was no stranger to inhabiting different forms—he was one of the true shapeshifters in the Nine Worlds after all. But shifting form was at his will and the form he chose. *But I drifted in the void in Ginnungagap too long. Am I too far from the Nine Worlds to wield my powers?* Memories stirred deeper within him. There was another being in the void—*that ancient awareness. Did she shape a new form when I could not? This form?*

Cautiously, Loki stood, testing the strength of his new body and adjusting to the differences in weight-bearing. He'd only transformed into women for short jests in the Nine Worlds, but this was could be much more perilous. *Can I shapeshift in this body at all?* There was something different, something missing. He wasn't sure what but it scratched at his consciousness, eluding attempts to come to the surface of his mind. What did matter right now was he'd escaped Freyja's cruses somehow. Whatever she'd intended for him, Loki was alive. Now all he needed is to reunite with Odin. "How am I supposed to do that? I don't even know where I am!"

Freyja had intended to destroy him but if she could see his predicament now, she'd surely find this more than enough cruel amusement.

"She always hated me. She'd love to see me stuck here … wherever here is."

Ignoring the problem he couldn't solve for the moment, Loki turned his attention to the one he could. *I'm still not tall but most of this height is legs.* Long, limber legs. He couldn't think of himself as *she*. *I'm not a woman. This body hasn't changed anything. I am still Loki.* But looking at the swell of small, firm breasts, and the curve of the hips, the auburn hair between his legs, this body was most definitely not masculine. *Identity is deeper than any flesh. I will always be Loki, no matter what form I take.*

He reached up to the top of his head and took a fistful of his long hair and inspected it. The tresses of hair twisted into fiery ringlets. *Still, I'm naked and the burning heat of the sun on bare, pale skin. I needed protection from the sun here or it'll will burn my skin.*

Behind Loki a fire was gaining strength. Smoke no longer curled lazily into the bright sky but many small sparse shrubs dotted the dunes where embers were already catching. A white sandy track led away between two dense, thorn-covered trees. *I'm caught between a fire and thorn trees. This mightn't be the Nine Worlds, but little has changed. Predicaments never favor me.*

I'm a child of Muspellheim, and I have an affinity with fire.

Loki lifted his hands palm up to face the fire, trying to calm the flames, but they singed the hairs on his arms and blistered the skin.

"Curse the Norns!" he shouted and pulled his hands back. He turned away and fled the fire through dense trees. Large thorns covered every branch and, wincing, even though shielding his face with his arms, he pushed through. The long thorns tore at his flesh and blood ran in hot rivulets down his bare arms.

Loki stumbled out the other side of the trees and swore. The skin on his arms was a ruin of burns and deep cuts. He winced. Now that the fire was behind him, the breeze against his bare skin was a fresh pain. Ahead, an ocean of turquoise waters stretched to the horizon. Here these icy-colored waters reminded him of the glaciers of Niflheim, but the breeze off the water was cool and not frigid. The water looked inviting against the heat of fire and sun. Loki stepped closer. He dipped a toe into the water. No frozen chill to it. Hesitantly, he bent lower and cupped the water in his hands. Despite the burns to his skin, the salt water only stung a little and the water was soothing.

Along the stretch of beach, the fire had advanced, flames consuming the brush and trees. He was trapped between the ocean and the flames, and Loki knew he couldn't stay there indefinitely. Searching along the coastline, he saw undulating sand hills in the distance. Beyond those were several hunched, stony forms of ancient red rock. The stone formations reminded him of trolls who'd been caught in the sunlight and transformed into rock. *Do they even have trolls here?* He'd never been lost in the Nine Worlds. Always the expert traveller but now he was lost and nothing was familiar.

Loki followed the beach to the red boulders. The sand beneath his bare feet was impossibly hot and he half ran, half hobbled across it, stopping frequently to bathe his burnt feet in the cool sea water. The sun was unbearable on his skin. He'd transformed into many beings over the eons of time, first a man, once a mare, a hawk, frequently a wolf, but he'd never been a woman before and was quite fond of his new form.

Glancing around, a narrow path led between the sand dunes. Without delay, he hurried across the beach, jogging through the sand dunes. The bellowing fire provided impetus to keep moving, and the extensive sand dunes would prevent the flames from getting too close. Even so, Loki ran down the winding track, the white sand soon giving way to red. The colors seemed foreboding in the fiery light, mingled together like blood and bone.

In the middle of the track, two spiny reptiles lifted clawed feet from the burning sand just as Loki had done running across the beach. *Are they mocking me?* They unfurled thorny headdresses from around their necks. The rattle of their spiked collars sent shivers of unease through him. They might be diminutive, but these creatures fiercely stood their ground against him.

Loki stopped in the centre the track, unease nagging him along with the sense of unseen eyes watching him. He turned, one hand raised to protect his eyes from the fire, but no one stood silhouetted against the blaze. On the other side of the track, the scrub land flowed in spiny bushes and finally large boulders. The place looked desolate. *How does anyone survive in this inhospitable land?* The sun turned an accusing glare on him again, and Loki's blistered skin ached beneath the harsh rays. *I need shelter.*

He scrambled up the side of a steep dune and ignored the hissing of the spiny lizards. He moved with eyes scrunched tight against the glare of the sun to the top of the dune. Unbalanced, he tipped and plunged down the other side. Plummeting, feet first, into empty air, Loki twisted cat-like as he fell and, rolling onto one shoulder, he landed hard on pebble-strewn soil.

Grit and sand sprayed outwards from his landing, but Loki didn't move. He wheezed in painful breaths and clutched at his ribs. A grimace of agony, then he rolled onto his back. He hesitated, cataloguing all the aches making themselves known but no sharp stabs like broken bones. When he was certain he'd not broken any ribs, and that only cuts, burns and scrapes covered his body, he eased into a sitting potion.

Loki placed his hands flat on the earth beside him. *Is that a pulse?* Closing his eyes, he concentrated on the earth beneath his palm. He felt it; the thrum of an ancient heart beating beneath the veins of the earth.

"Norns, where am I?"

"Your crones were only children when this country was made, fire-child." The light but firm voice said from behind him.

Startled, Loki turned. Squinting against the billowing smoke plumes that covered the horizon, he saw a woman silhouetted against the fiery sky. She was long-legged and stood with feet apart, toes sunk deep into the sand. Although she seemed middle-aged, a spear was in one hand, and the lines etched on her face were made from smiles and laughter, not bitterness or anger.

"You're far from your homelands, fire-child."

"Where exactly is *here?* I'm Loki, not 'fire-child.' What might I call you?"

"Anjea. This is my country. I'm the one who gave you breath and form when you were cast adrift, Loki." She breathed his name on the wind and in response to his true nature, a fiery gust of embers swirled around them.

"You transformed me? Gave me this body?"

"You've sustained more injuries than you realize. Rest here and I will get what aid you need."

She walked to him, covering the distance in a matter of a few strides. Weariness pressed down on him and although he fought it, the compulsion to sleep was too strong. Loki flinched as Anjea reached for him, taking his blistered hands gently in her own. He'd not realized how badly the skin had blistered and was raw and bleeding where he'd scraped it rolling across the ground. But there was something much worse. There was a far deeper, soul-breaking injury.

Anjea sat beside him, held him against her like a distraught child. Loki fought it but his essence leeched from this new body. His very nature, the power of a fire giant and a being even the Aesir gods had feared. And now it was fading like blood spilling from a wound. Anjea cradled him closer and Loki closed his eyes. He relaxed into her arms despite the unfamiliar words of her song: it was a soothing rhythm like the slow beating of a heart.

Dark Dreams

Darkness swallowed him. In the shifting shadows, forms seemed to waver, contorting into half-formed figures. *Is someone there?* He strained his senses, fearing movement in the darkness. Fearing that someone else was here with him. He twisted his head from left to right, trying to peer into the inky blackness. *Norns curse me, where am I?* Again, Loki had a vague sense of movement in the darkness, a shifting in the shadows, but then nothing. His heartbeat echoed in the silence, beating louder than any war drum. Closing his eyes, Loki focused on the rhythm of his heart. This was the only certainty, his only guidance in the dark. Wordlessly, he prayed to the Norns, those wretched crones, that this was just a horrible dream.

He drifted, half-awake but conscious of his heartbeat. They'd bound his hands at the wrists, iron manacles securing them to the stone plinth. A thick chain ran across his chest and another set of manacles bound his ankles to the rock. He strained against the iron band that pinned his throat, too, the purpose of such a restraint not yet revealed.

He knew why he was there. Odin had pronounced his fate for his affair with the witch Angrboda, they'd been a doomed couple and their children also taken from them. But Loki had found some kindred flame with Angrboda and beneath those tangled branches of the Iron Wood, they had loved one another, understood one another. But unbeknown to Loki, Angrboda had shared Gullveig's lineage of witches, and Odin would not tolerate their brood to live. So, Loki had taken Odin's favorite son from him. The bright and beloved Baldr, the golden one among the

Aesir. Now Odin had bound him in punishment, but it was a torture not yet fulfilled.

Loki touched the tip of his tongue to the air, tasting the faint sulfurous tang. As a child of Muspellheim, he had spent much of his life underground, wretched, and alone. He had marveled at Odin and his kin, at how skilful and dexterous their bodies compared to his own stunted, twisted form.

Odin had offered Loki a quick and lithe body, one that could match his sharp wit and tongue. He'd desired nothing more than to be beside Odin. The All-Father had always known him so well. Odin had always seen through Loki's lies. How grand a jest it must have been to transform such a lonely creature as Loki into a being as quick of body as mind. How foolish Loki had been even then to think there was no ulterior motive behind Odin's actions. In binding Loki to him, calling him brother and bound by a blood-pledge, together they had made Asgard and the golden hall of Valhalla, with Loki's place secured by Odin's side forever.

Loki jerked as light flickered on the periphery of his sight. Turning his head as quickly as the iron restraints would allow, shadows fled from the lantern light. Chained by unbreakable dwarf-forged restraints riveted to the stone beneath him, Loki arched his body towards the light. It was basic instinct—the need for warmth and light. Peering through the shadows, he could make out a slender cloaked figure, lantern held high as they continued cautiously but steadily into the cavern.

"Help me," Loki called.

The cloaked woman shook her head, pale blonde hair like moonlight in the darkness.

"It's forbidden, my love. But I will do what I can for you," she said, her voice soft and sorrowful.

Sigyn. My wife, my faithful wife Odin insisted I marry. Sigyn, dutiful unto my very end.

"Who forbids you to free your husband?" he asked as he tested his strength against the iron fetters again. It did little good. There was not even the slightest bend in the metal.

"Odin gives the orders."

"Is Odin your husband now? To whom do you owe your loyalty and devotion, Sigyn?"

"That's unkind of you." She sat and bowed her head beside him.

"Cursed Norns, of course it's unkind of me! He binds me here because he knows what his arrogance and pride have wrought him."

"You angered many."

Loki frowned. He followed Sigyn's eyes as they flicked to the shadows behind her. *Is she afraid? Is there someone else here? Is this more than reluctance to save her traitorous husband?* Sigyn's eyes widened and her hand tremored.

"Come out and face me. Stop lurking in the darkness," he demanded.

"It was never just Odin you wronged," a cold voice said. "But perhaps you're more like the Aesir than you realize. You've forgotten our kind hold grudges."

"Ah, Skadi. You imagine yourself wronged by me too?"

Skadi strode from the darkness and stepped into the circle of light cast by Sigyn's lantern. A cold malice radiated from Skadi and her pale blonde hair was bound in warrior braids, her ice-blue eyes as piercing as always.

"Skadi." Loki greeted her with a grimace.

"Loki." The frost giantess acknowledged him with a slight smile.

"Whatever wrongs I committed against you and those of Jotunheim were at the behest of Odin."

"Yet Odin allows me vengeance against you."

Moving with deliberate care, she took something from a leather pouch at her hip. The shimmer of scales was all Loki could see. He twisted in his bonds as she reached up for the chains hanging down above his head.

"You needn't do this."

"Correct. But I want to. I want my name to be the last thing you scream into the darkness of this world."

Skadi found the iron chains hanging from the cavern ceiling and turned a cruel smile on Loki. She showed him the pale blue scales of the mountain viper coiled in the palm of her gloved hand. His eyes widened, and he thrashed. The venom of the smallest snake in Jotunheim burned like hoarfrost and rotted flesh like the bitterest of mountain winds.

"You can't do this," he begged. He strained against the fetters on his wrists and ankles, twisting beneath the chains looped across his hips and chest. Worse still was the cold steel at his throat, the one that held his head against the stone.

"Odin gave me his blessing. This is my vengeance for the death of Thjazi. He was more than the king of Jotunheim, Loki. He was my father."

"Your father acted on his own. Are you sure you're not just punishing me for making you laugh when you married old Njord? Making a fool of Thjazi's daughter and queen of Jotunheim?"

"You lied and cheated my father. I am not so petty that my marriage with Njord would be worthy of this revenge against you. I am a giant. I you remembered who you were once, you'd know that giants aren't like Odin and his trivial Aesir."

Skadi moved slowly, reaching up to loop the viper through the chain above Loki's head. He stilled, watching in terror as the scaled form uncoiled and it fixed its pale gaze on him.

"Skadi!" Loki pleaded.

She shook her head in disappointment and brushed past Sigyn without further comment. Skadi strode from the cavern, darkness engulfing her. Before he could speak to his wife, pain flared across his right cheek, and he screamed. Quickly, he tried to jerk his face away, but the manacle around his throat held his head in place as a second drop of the viper's poison landed on the edge of his jaw. The agony was worse than Loki had imagined, burning deeper than frost or flame. His body arched against the pain, tears brimming in his eyes that trickled down his cheeks, the salt searing his burns.

Sigyn rushed to his side, smoothing back his sweaty brow, removing the hair from his eyes. Loki gritted his teeth against the pain, counting heartbeats until another drop of venom fell from the viper's fangs. Kneeling beside him, Sigyn lifted a shallow clay bowl she had kept hidden in the folds of her cloak. Loki glanced at her, eyes widening with the realization she had deliberately deceived Skadi and disobeyed Odin. He whispered his thanks as she lifted the bowl into position, catching the next drop of venom. Loki focused on the swelling venom on the tip of the viper's fangs before the droplet hung, suspended for what might have been an eternity before it fell neatly into the bowl Sigyn held above his face. Weakly, Loki exhaled and blessed her, his rasping voice an echo in the silence.

Painted Serpents

Loki followed the rhythm of his heartbeat, dragging him back to consciousness and into his body. Agony greeted him, the fragility of his body burning with fever and making the bitter terror of his dreams seem like a balm to his mind. *Oh Norns, you cursed hags!* He knew the sisters were not kind sculptors of Fate. Their shears often cut the threads of mortality without mercy, but they had always bound his flesh and shade.

Hesitantly, he opened his eyes, already suspecting the scars that would greet him. His body felt cut, abraded, and burnt. As he expected, his hands were a raised network of scars, his skin covered in abrasions and burns. *Where am I?* His mind still felt clouded, reality and memory a tangle of images. The beach. *Was that real? Or dreamscape?* The woman with skin the colour of night sky, eyes like a cosmos. *Was she real? Or a figment of his imagination?* He remembered her song. It had reverberated with his entire being like a plucked harp string. She had been real. He knew she could be no less. *Anjea.*

He closed his eyes again, conscious of the fever burning his flesh from within. Wherever he was now, the air was stale, sickness leeching from his body like a miasma. He was not sure he could trust this new form. His power felt like it was pulling his flesh apart, and he half expected the puckered scars crisscrossing his body to break open. *Was this new body able to contain the raw power of Muspellheim's fire giants? Did this new world even have such beings?* His transformation felt only half-completed, as though he were a parasite clinging to this flesh, obstinately separate and unable to integrate with this new shape. *If I don't act, I cannot heal or live.* He knew what needed to be done, but it was a terrible choice. But when had his choices ever been good?

Loki knew the only way he could survive long enough to seek retribution from Freyja was to bury his fiery heart of the fire giant. Once he took this action, only Odin would have the strength and skill to reunite his shattered pieces later, so Loki prayed to the Norns that Freyja had not cursed Odin too. Inhaling, he turned his gaze internally, shrinking that fiery strength of his power to the smallest of embers. When the power Odin had granted him was barely glowing coal, Loki forged it into a lava stone. While it kept the heat of his power, he inscribed a single rune on its surface. The sigil of his name. Then, he closed his awareness of the lava stone and withdrew from the depths of his mind and back to the awareness of his body.

He sucked in a breath of pain. The denial of himself was as sharp as a cut, but it was temporary. Without the energy this new body expended containing his power, its reserves of strength flowed to heal cuts and burns. He trembled, biting down hard on his lip, the coppery taste of blood filling his mouth. He was weak, made mortal in this flesh and its fragility overwhelmed him.

Loki tried and failed to open his eyelids but they fluttered weakly. He exhaled shakily, aware of movement around him and whispers nearby. Pain seared along his nerves, and he doubled over, clutching at his abdomen. Breathing in quick gasps, fever sent shivers through him. *Odin find me. Please find me soon.* Fear flooded him and perspiration drenched him. He hoped Odin had managed to outwit Freyja and uncovered her treachery before the cycle of Ragnarök could begin again. But his greatest fear now was that Odin had been as blind as he had and, in being so focused on destroying each other, they'd missed Freyja manoeuvring unseen in the shadows.

Time drifted, passed, and coalesced. It could have been moments or days later when Loki finally woke again. Forcing his eyelids open, the brightness of the firelight was dazzling. Momentarily blinded, Loki blinked rapidly, struggling to focus as movement blurred into indistinct shapes. Fighting dizziness two golden pinpoints were clear. There was the scuff of quiet feet on stone, the rustle of clothing as someone moved to his side.

"You're awake, fire-child." A woman's voice that was familiar, like Anjea's but not quite the same. Trying to focus, Loki looked at the golden hue of the stone walls. There was a warmth to them that had been absent in the black stone of the caverns of Svartalfaheim. Loki shivered at the dream—his memory—bound and tortured before the final days of Ragnarök began. Slowly, Loki relaxed under the glow of the cavern walls and the firelight flickering along them. His gaze sharpened, noticing the painted designs decorating the walls and ceiling. An unbidden trickle of fear shivered through him.

Painted serpentine forms shifted in firelight across the cave walls. Intricate designs covered their sinuous bodies. The bright colors of their scales in the firelight made them shimmer, appearing to writhe across the stone. His heart pounding, the serpents flexed, coils loosening, forked tongues flicking at him.

Memory of the ice viper Skadi had tortured him with overwhelmed Loki's mind. He threw back the furs, limbs tangling in the blankets as he staggered to his feet. The chamber floor lurched horribly beneath him, but Loki grabbed instinctively for something to stop his fall. Despite his parched throat and cracked lips, Loki screamed. He staggered and fell, horribly weak. The impact with the floor sent pain rocketing through him. Darkness swam at the edges of his sight, and he swayed. Strong arms caught him from behind, lowering him to the floor.

Loki writhed in the grip that held him. "Odin. Odin!"

He continued to spit curses, punching and kicking at the restraining hands until he felt his foot strike someone's jaw. The hands holding him suddenly withdrew with a quiet curse.

"Baiame, she's like an angry dingo," a man snarled.

Loki spun and twisted upright. His sight was still blurry, his heart tripping with fear, but he lifted his fists in a defensive posture.

A tall man stood in front of him, massaging his jaw. He had a wild tangle of black hair around his head and shoulders. Unfamiliar swirls and symbols decorated his broad chest, his skin the deep colour of the night sky. Glancing wildly around the cavern, Loki found he recognised nothing. Fever dragged at him, weakening his limbs, and his arms trembled. The ground rose beneath him again and he stumbled. The tall stranger moved forward, taking Loki's arms, and lifted him bodily onto the hard pallet covered in furs.

The man turned to someone in the shadows. "Are you certain she's not dingo kin? She fights like them."

Loki struggled, trying to rise, but the man effortlessly held him pinned to the bed.

"She's not of the dingo kin. Not even from Country, Wahn. As I've already told you, if you'd been listening, there's a connection between that furious fire storm and this fire-child. Now, can you hold her for me?"

"She bites."

The woman *tsked*, and the shadow of the man fell over Loki. He applied only slight pressure to his wrists, but Loki breathed deeply, willing himself to calm down. *She? I did not imagine my transformation then.*

"Loki?"

The older woman leaned over the bed, her power wrapping around him like a cloak. It was soothing, his panic disappearing as easily as if she had set a poultice to a wound. Holding his gaze, Loki stared into her ageless face. She reminded him strongly of Anjea with her eyes like a cosmos. This woman had golden eyes that shone like twin moons. Loki licked his cracked lips, wincing.

"Anjea?" he asked.

"I'm Yhi. Anjea brought you to me for healing. You need to rest now but you're safe here, fire-child."

Loki struggled to sit upright, but the man's hands restrained him. "I need to find Odin."

"You need to heal before you can go anywhere."

Loki twisted, desperate to make them understand. "Find Odin."

"Your kind have never walked on Country before, but Anjea is a skilled crafter and she's made your form for this place. You just need to rest before you go on whatever journey brings you to us."

"This isn't right." Loki moved his legs, flapping his hands uselessly despite the man holding him down.

Loki felt the cool touch on his brow again, soothing away his fears and leaving a sense of reassurance. He watched the woman called Yhi carefully brush a long auburn curl from his cheek. Loki smiled. The Aesir had all desired Baldr's golden locks and Loki had been no different. But now he had his own fiery curls. He felt an odd sense of smugness about that. *Perhaps this transformation is not so terrible after all?*

"Wahn will guard you while you rest. Anjea might be a fine crafter of flesh, but I am the healer here."

Loki glanced at the man called Wahn. He had removed his hands from Loki's wrists and stepped back to the edge of the cavern. He seemed more comfortable there, away from the centre of attention, hidden among the shadows. Loki could understand that. He, too, had always been more at ease away from the firelight. There was an inexplicable kinship with this stranger, but trying to catch his eyes, Loki found Wahn's dark gaze always avoided him. *Curious.* He would get the answers he needed, but, for now, Loki relaxed into the furs of the bed, watching the healer's golden eyes as she administered the various ointments and balms to his cuts, burns and scrapes.

Loki returned his gaze to the cavern walls, but the painted serpents had stilled. The multihued scales had stopped writhing, and those bright eyes now blinked lazily, tongues flicking in satiation, fangs no longer bared. Allowing the healing sleep to take him, Loki dreamed of slaking his vengeance with Freyja's blood. When he woke, he would get the answers he needed and find Odin.

25

FRIEND OR FOE

The underground chamber was the same when Loki woke. Hesitantly, he flexed his fingers, testing how well the skin had healed. There was no pain anymore and his fever seemed to have disappeared during his sleep. He could say one thing about Yhi. She was a magnificent healer. There was an unpleasant smell of stale sweat that clung to his body, and he longed to bathe. Looking around the cavern, he realised he was alone. *Where is Yhi? Where is that shadowy figure, Wahn?*

"You're awake, fire-child." Wahn sat in the dimly lit corner of the chamber.

Loki peered at him. The shadows wrapped themselves around Wahn, making his features hard to discern. What was visible was the wildly curling hair, the colour of darkest night.

"My name's Loki, not 'fire-child' as you keep calling me."

Wahn shrugged and stepped from the shadows. Up close, he was mesmerising. His bare chest was painted in strange sigils Loki didn't recognise and bright, intelligent eyes took in everything from behind a prominent nose. Loki felt an inexplicable connection. What power was Wahn using to make Loki feel this bond with him? That was a dangerous magic and he could ill-afford to be ensnared by it.

Wahn met Loki's eyes. "I'm told to make sure you rest."

"I'll keep that in mind."

Loki sat up slowly, ignoring the dizziness as he moved. There wasn't any pain anymore, but he was still very weak. Despite this, he swung his legs over the edge of the stone shelf he'd been sleeping on and breathed shallowly but steadily.

"These actions would be contrary to the instructions Yhi gave me," Wahn noted but didn't move to stop Loki.

"Are you going to stop me?"

Wahn shrugged one muscular shoulder. "If *you* want to be stupid, I'll not stop you."

Loki pushed to his feet. The cavern walls lurched horribly and the ground tilted sharply beneath his bare feet. He dug his toes into the soft sand, attempting to anchor himself. I *won't collapse like a weakling. I am not going back to my sickbed like a cripple.* Sweat ran down his face and he shuffled a few steps forward. His eyesight blurred but he still saw Wahn's mocking smile as Wahn's firm hands gripped his shoulders, catching him just as his knees buckled. *Norns curse me, Wahn's amused by this.*

Loki's heartbeat fluttered like a caged bird within his ribs and Wahn easily picked him up and, without comment, deposited him on the pile of furs. Loki's head flopped back and he closed his eyes, trying to calm his erratic pulse.

"I think that is precisely why you're supposed to rest," Wahn said with a smug smile.

"Are you my nursemaid, then?"

"I'm told you're important, though I'm yet to see a reason for that."

"You don't like me very much, do you?"

"You take foolish risks."

"You don't like me much. I'm usually charming to both men and women."

"Then your Country is in a woeful place."

"It is. But that's why I need to find Odin and set things right. Restore what should be and not whatever Freyja has done."

"When in fever-dreams you spoke of Odin. Who is he to you?"

"Odin's my brother, a warrior. But something terrible happened, a curse, I think. Now I'm here and I hope he's still in Valhalla planning how to reunite us and not … cast into the Ginnungagap as I was."

Wahn's eyes narrowed. "And how *did* you come to be here?"

"I'm no threat to you or this world. I don't even possess my powers here. I'm mortal and this form, while very pleasing, isn't the one I need of fire and might."

"Yhi and Anjea suspect you hid your power somehow. That's guilty action, Loki."

"Well, it wasn't guilt," Loki snapped. "My power's made from the fires of the Muspellheim itself. This flesh can't contain it. I mean no insult to Anjea, and she crafted a magnificent body for me, but it was being destroyed by what I am."

Wahn cocked an eyebrow. "And so, you hid your true power from us?"

"Why are you determined that I'm guilty of something?"

"Trust isn't my virtue, but its absence has kept me alive this long. You're a stranger here and your kind have never walked on Country before. As soon as you can stand upright by yourself, I'll make certain we return you to your Nine Worlds."

Loki paled. "I can't travel back through Ginnungagap again."

He frowned. "What is this thing you call Ginnungagap?"

"You don't know Ginnungagap? It's the primordial darkness between the Nine Worlds and … wherever I am now."

"Ah, we have another name for that starless expanse. Loki, I don't much care how you return, I only care that you do."

"You really don't like me, do you?"

"There is great instability in having two Tricksters in this cosmos."

"Tricksters?"

"We're both Tricksters, Loki. You aren't so stupid as to not notice the bond we share. You're like me, a kindred being."

"I'm nothing like you. Who are you in the scheme of things here?"

"I'm Wahn. I am the Crow, the *schemer* but sometimes a helper. Only Yhi and Anjea really appreciate my importance though."

"I know that feeling."

"Anjea is a skilled craftswoman, but there are more far-reaching concerns in you being here."

"What can be worse than being powerless?"

"Without true bonds to Country, you can't draw strength from its waters, nor benefit from the bounties that should nourish you. Your mortal body will slowly fade."

"Curse the Norns. I'm going to die, aren't I?"

"Are these Norns responsible for why you're here?"

"No. Before Ginnungagap, I was dying after the battle at Ragnarök. Freyja found me and cursed me."

"Is Freyja a friend or an enemy?"

"She was Odin's ally, but that doesn't mean she was any friend of mine. Events leading to Ragnarök and the battle itself were between Odin and me. They were a little complicated."

"A lot of complications are associated with you. Nor do you lack for enemies. What makes you certain Odin was not false like Freyja?"

Loki glared at Wahn. "Odin and I are brothers. Our binding surpasses all disagreements, all battles, and, eventually, every outcome. Our cosmos, the Nine Worlds are cyclical and events play out each time with slight shifts in the pattern, but the outcome is always the same. Odin and I fight, we die and then Ginnungagap consumes all and renewal begins the cycle again. Never has there been a Nine Worlds without me and Odin in it. Whatever Freyja has done could have implications well beyond her anticipation."

Yhi entered from the narrow tunnel at the rear of the cavern. Loki hadn't seen her use any other passage. "Odin is powerful in the Nine Worlds?"

"He is the most powerful."

"Then we must summon him to help reunite you with the Nine Worlds."

"That isn't a simple task," Wahn said.

"No, and yet it's what must be done. Weren't you just complaining about how Loki is a danger to Country?"

Wahn crossed his arms over his muscular chest. "He is."

"His arrival on Country was not by mistake. Anjea found him lost in the darkness and summoned his shade here. So, we must use a similar force to draw Odin to Country."

Wahn pursed his lips. "That is more reckless than anything I have ever devised."

"Which is why you must keep him safe and then help Anjea and me summon Odin. You have particular skills suited to this task."

"I'm not a nursemaid."

"And I'm not a child," Loki said.

Wahn glared at him. "Be polite and remember, you're mortal here."

Yhi settled herself by the firepit. "There are dangers that are beyond my control, Loki. Wahn will be vigilant, but don't rely on him."

Loki thought the man would protest, but he merely shrugged as though the insult did not reflect poorly on him. While he considered what to say, how to object to being treated like a fool, he noticed Yhi was preparing nuts into a mash, Wahn skinning a small furry animal. His stomach growled in anticipation of food, and Loki decided he would wait until after the meal to raise any complaints. He yawned, stretching out on the furs. The temperature inside the cavern was warm, with the fire flaring high. Loki laid his head down on the bundled furs he was using for a pillow and let his thoughts wonder about how he might have earned Freyja's hatred.

THE RAINBOW SERPENT

In the underground chamber, time was meaningless to Loki. He didn't know how long he'd been on Country. When Yhi was absent, which was frequent, Wahn kept watch on Loki. Desperate to do more than stretch his limbs within the confines of the cavern, Loki wanted to explore. Wahn cautioned him against such recklessness, reminding him he was mortal now, his body fading even if he didn't feel it yet. But he'd never been restrained before.

When the time finally came that Wahn needed to be elsewhere, Loki agreed to stay within the chamber until Wahn or Yhi returned soon. But, true to his nature as a liar, the moment Wahn left, Loki leapt to his feet. He ventured into the narrow passage he'd always seen Yhi use. It was very narrow, but his body was a slight feminine form now, and he eagerly walked into the darkness.

The passage twisted and turned into itself, a labyrinth of turns that Loki soon forgot. It was only a single passage, curling through the earth like a snake. It made Loki nervous to think of a serpentine dragon living underground down here. *Did Country have a being like Nidhöggr? Am I going to find a devourer of corpses at the end of this tunnel?* He hoped not. Even at the terrifying thought of snake and dragons, his pulse beat quickly with excitement. *I'm finally free.*

The ground of the tunnel sloped downwards, his bare feet scuffing pebbles loose from the path he followed. They rolled down the passage, bouncing off the tunnel walls and continuing beyond his sight. Although it was dark, Loki had spent enough time in the poorly lit gloom to see enough in the darkness. He was surprised when the passage ended abruptly, opening into a cavernous space instead.

Edging forward along the path, Loki saw a deep pool of water in the middle of the space. *Is it an underground lake?* Looking up, Loki couldn't see any hint of sky or sunlight. He was deep underground then. Turning his attention back to the pool, his eyes followed a brief movement in the water. His unease heightened. There was an awareness to this place, too, as though he were being watched. And with dreadful realization, Loki knew he wasn't alone.

Loki's gaze flicked from the shadows gathered in the crevasses of the cavern walls to the faint light from the pool. Phosphorescence in the water illuminated the cavern, but Loki felt no desire to explore. He glanced back to the tunnel he had followed. There was no one there. Whatever the other presence was in the chamber, it was growing stronger and closer.

"I'll leave here now. I'm aware you're angry at my trespass."

Glancing hurriedly at the turquoise-colored water, Loki frowned. Where he'd thought there was a movement before, there was now a ripple across the surface of the pool. Stepping quickly away from the edge of the rocky precipice where he stood, Loki felt the gathering menace in the chamber with him. He might not possess his powers anymore, but mortals had always felt the presence of gods. Loki knew he was in the presence of an ancient being, and one not benevolently inclined to him.

A massive form reared from the depths of the pool, slapping waves against the cavern walls. Loki stumbling backwards so fast he tripped and fell against the side of one wall. Huddled on the ground, he stared at the many-hued coils of the massive snake.

The enormous being reminded Loki of its smaller kin he'd seen depicted on the cavern walls of Yhi's chamber. Those little serpents hadn't liked him either. Warily, Loki met the fierce intellect in that gaze. He recoiled immediately from the lightning that lit those reptilian eyes.

"My trespass was unintended." Loki cowered, pressing himself against the stone wall, never more aware of his mortality than now.

The massive coils of the serpent's body writhed in the water, and Loki saw the tail lashing in agitation.

"You are not of this Country."

"I'm not. I was lost beyond the starless expanse. Anjea gave my shade form, and Yhi healed my flesh. I want only to return to my Worlds."

"I am Yurlunggul. I've never heard of Loki before. But you've the taste of one known to me. Are you not Wahn in disguise? Such tricks won't work on me, little crow."

"I'm not Wahn," Loki said, terrified. *What has that wretched man done to this being? How much trouble am I in because of him?*

Yurlunggul reared back, horned head nearly hitting the rocky ceiling above. Loki pushed himself off the stone wall, hoping to flee the chamber at the first opportunity.

"I do not favour Wahn and his trickery," Yurlunggul said.

"I don't favour him either. But he has promised to help return me to my Worlds. Would that not please you? The sooner I leave, the sooner I am not on Country?"

Yurlunggul twisted its head to regard him, silver eyes pinning him with a fierce intensity. "Tell Wahn to hasten his plans or I will come for him."

Loki nodded jerkily and scooted from the chamber, the roar of the rainbow-coloured serpent following him as he fled through the passages, stones shaking loose with the fury of his rage.

Loki ran in the blind terror, hurrying through the dark passages that he had cautiously traversed earlier. His bare feet bruised on the many small stones, sharp edges of the rock opening tiny cuts. He continued, heedless of the pain, heart hammering, ignoring the cuts that traversed the soles of his feet. He thought only of escape from this endless underground warren. *I need to see the sky, feel the breeze.* The stale air of the underground and overwhelming claustrophobia drove Loki to keep running, bloody footprints in his wake.

The slope of the passage floor tilted upwards and Loki's breathing steadied, the panic slowly leeching from him. *I've been underground too long. I can't be underground.* Memories of being bound beneath the black rock of Svartalfaheim, Skadi's cruel torture and Odin's callous words. Countless days and endless nights of torture. In those times, Skadi had come for vengeance against him. But Freyja had moved in the shadows, never openly. Freyja had been sly for all her use of his nickname among the Aesir. They had called him the 'Sly One', which had always seemed ridiculous to him considering how the Aesir conducted themselves. But Freyja had outmanoeuvred him all the same.

The ground suddenly sloped upward in a steep incline and Loki sped up. His rasping breath echoed in the silence, his footsteps following the same rapid rhythm as his heartbeat. Still fearful of the malevolence Yurlunggul had shown him, Loki struggled through the sandy soil and loose pebbles that rolled beneath his feet. Racing up the incline, Loki saw the end of the tunnel, the arched golden stone of the opening. Beyond was the night sky and millions of stars. Desperate to be beneath that sky, Loki ran on shaking legs, wincing as his toes gripped the edge and the momentum of his flight propelled him forward and over the lip of the tunnel opening.

A steep drop waited on the other side. Loki's heart stuttered as he hung, suspended in open air, before gravity dragged him back to the earth. He tumbled, starry sky and red sand inverting round and round as Loki rolled down the slope, gathering speed the further he was from the cave entrance. He came to a sudden stop, shoulders slamming painfully against a large boulder. Cursing viciously with a painful gasp, Loki uncurled his bruised body. He lay still on his back, tears pricked his eyes, the relief of freedom, fresh air filling his lungs.

The night sky was a black dome that arched above him, a dense scattering of stars unfamiliar to him. *Everything is strange here.* But it did not matter. He was no longer trapped within the earth. But even as he enjoyed the first moments of freedom, his mind returned traitorously to Yurlunggul, and the threat issued. If Loki did not leave Country as fast Yurlunggul wanted, the rainbow serpent would extinguish him. It seemed the only way to avoid obliteration and see his vengeance slaked in the Nine Worlds was to accept Wahn's help.

THE CROW

Sitting up, Loki rubbed his bruised shoulder. Finally, he looked around at his surroundings, noticing the fine red sand covering the ground. It was finer than the black sand beaches in the Nine Worlds, finer even than the white sand beaches he had encountered when he first arrived in this strange Country. Crushing the sand between his fingers, red grit stained his pale hands. This was nothing like the Nine Worlds. It was a wonder and marvel of its own. *How was Yhi going to summon Odin to this cosmos? And can I trust Wahn? He doesn't seem like anyone I'd confide in. He reminds me too much of myself.*

"This is all strategy. I need Odin's mind and guidance."

Loki staggered to his feet, hissing with pain. Grimacing, he inspected the soles of his feet, trying to see how badly he might have ruined them in his panicked escape. Minor cuts covered his feet, with gouges where the flesh had been carved out by tiny stone flakes. Walking was going to be horrendous. *But I need to think. I do that best while moving.*

Starting forward in an awkward shuffle, Loki continued across the warm sand underfoot which retained heat even in the darkest hours of the night. He didn't intend to walk far but enough to explore some of the surrounding land. *Surely there's no harm in that while I think.*

Strange fibrous plants grew in dense clusters from the uneven, sandy ground and there were more large boulders, harsh-looking plants. It reminded him of the lava fields and stony slopes of the mountains in Midgard. *Humanity thrived there when only moss would grow on those stones. Why would here be any less likely? What are the mortals of Country like?* He had always found mortals fascinating.

Intrigued by the landscape, Loki turned his gaze upward again. Countless stars filled the sky, but there was a wonder running through it all. Stardust gathered in a painted landscape looking like a river through the night sky. But on the very horizon, much brighter than any other star, a constellation beckoned to him. Focusing on the brightest star closest to the horizon, Loki started walking after it.

The night was deep around him, heavy with the peaceful silence of early morning. Already Loki could see the first touch of daylight on the horizon, the glow of golden sunlight leeching the brilliance from the night sky and the star Loki had been following. He stopped, standing in the absolute quiet of the desert. The divide between sky and land made clearer through the golden slash of dawn against darkness. Sudden exhaustion threatened to overwhelm him, and Loki trembled. *How far have I walked from Yhi's cavern?*

He dropped weakly to his knees, unable to bear his weight any longer. Raucous laughter erupted from a cluster of spiky plants. Above the unfriendly looking vegetation, sharp leaves resembling sword blades arched into the sky. A large black bird cocked its head at him, eying him dubiously. It reminded Loki a little of Odin's two ravens, Huginn and Muninn, but there was fierce intelligence in its gaze and mockery too. This was not a raven like Odin's two birds. The plumage was still ebony black, but it was slightly smaller than any of the ravens in the Nine Worlds, and it lacked the denser feathers beneath its beak.

"What are you then?" Loki asked. "A good omen or a bad one?"

The bird tilted its head one way and then the other way, the gesture slightly mocking. Then it hopped closer to Loki, moving along the thin branch it perched upon. The white bark of the scraggly tree was striking against the blue sky. *How does anything survive here?*

"Well then? I'm lost. Want to help me find my way?"

The bird cawed, a voice so like a raven that Loki started.

"What're you then? I know you're no ordinary bird. I'm not that much of a fool."

The bird cocked its head again, considering. It opened its wings, flapped them for two consecutive beats until it was aloft, then dropped to the ground near Loki. Still fixing him with its unblinking stare, the bird hopped sideways to Loki for a few paces, then cawed again. A noisy, mocking rebuke.

"Well, I'd get 'unlost' promptly if I could, but I can't even leave this Country on my own. I've been threatened by an incredibly hostile and enormous snake already tonight and now I'm lost. It's very plain to me, I'm as unwelcome here as I am in my own Worlds."

The bird cawed louder, and Loki heard a definite insult in its harsh tone.

"You don't like me either, then?" Loki gestured rudely at the bird. Sighing, he stared at the sun shining crimson on the horizon and closed his eyes. The night had been a mistake.

Loki's eyes were still closed when the desert woke around him with the sunrise. It felt as though the touch of light upon the sand was magic of its own. Opening his eyes, Loki stared at the bloody rays that were splayed across the red sand and felt a keen longing for snow. He'd always hated the cold of Jotunheim, the deadly embrace of Niflheim and the bitterness of Svartalfaheim. But now he missed those worlds. He even missed the lava fields of Muspellheim and the green hills of Asgard. Without him and Odin there, the Nine Worlds would collapse into imbalance—the fibre of the Nine Worlds decaying and breaking apart. *Did Freyja realize this when she cursed me? Did she know what calamity she had invoked?*

Exhausted and homesick, Loki felt the strength Yhi and Anjea had instilled in him failing. Was there any point trying to save himself from the scorching sun? Already those fiery fingers were reaching across the desert and soon the harsh sunlight would bathe the desert in its heat. Loki huddled on the ground, glaring reproachfully at the bird that watched him with uncanny intelligence and waited for the sun.

THE SEVEN STARS

Loki woke under the full heat of the sun. His skin felt drawn tight across his body and heat radiated from him as though he burned with fever again. Prying his eyes open, eyelids stuck together from crusted tears, he blinked in the daylight. The brightness of the sun was blinding. But that was not what had woken him. He could hear voices murmuring nearby. Struggling to move his cramped limbs, pain lanced through him and made him gasp. *I need to be more careful with this mortal flesh, or it'll never survive.* Loki squinted. *Where were the voices coming from?* He shivered. There were only stunted plants and taller, straggly shrubs. Not wanting to draw attention to himself, Loki slowly shifted his aching limbs until he was sure he could try standing. The whispered argument continued nearby, but no one paid any attention to him. *Perhaps they don't even know I'm here?*

The sun was a swollen, white-gold inferno in the sky. Despite it being early morning, Loki's skin had already burnt scarlet. *How can anyone spend a day beneath beneath this sun?* He needed to find shelter before his phantom imagining was reality.

Scanning the vicinity, a white straggly tree with a bird perched upon it was directly in his path. He shook his head as though to dislodge the hallucination. *When did I move? Am I so disoriented that the tree wasn't on the horizon behind me?* Or have I got turned around? At sunrise there'd been no tree as sunlight spread across the desert. Loki half turned to see several other white-barked trees in the near distance but all were behind him except for this one now in his path. *What in the Nine Worlds is happening?*

He looked more closely at the tree. An animal pelt draped across the sparse canopy, creating a shelter with more furs piled beneath the shade.

A strident voice nearby broke through a hushed argument. Loki stilled. A clamor of voices began talking at once, and he flinched at the noise they made in the quiet desert. If he listened carefully, he could hear the faint sound of splashing water. *Is there a river nearby? A lake or pond?* There'd been nothing like that as he followed the stars last night. But he was suddenly very thirsty. He followed the sound of voices, pushing through the pain and trembling in his legs as the muscles cramped with the effort.

Through the cluster of white-bark trees, seven women walked towards him, their steps in unison. He stared at their undeniable beauty, the symmetry of movement, but also at how similar they all were to each other. *Sisters.* He wet his cracked lips, thirst forgotten for something more primal. He might be in female form now, but desire still aroused at the sight of these seven magnificent women. A familiar caw broke the silence from the tree where the shelter had been.

"Wahn has returned," one of women informed her siblings.

She had a determined stride that brought her closer to Loki. But she hesitated on finding him awake and moving towards her. She stooped to the ground and picked up a large rock, hefting it in one hand. Loki put his arms up in placation, but the stone soared past him aimed at the large black crow in the tree above.

The bird lifted into the air with an indignant caw, wings flapping slowly as it circled the area, not willing to land too near the sisters but not willing to leave either. The woman approached, and Loki hesitantly met her eyes. Seven stars rotated in the depths of her pupils. Startled, Loki lurched backward, but she ignored his shock and took two deliberate steps toward him. Squatting down, she reached out a hand and plucked at Loki's ringleted red hair.

"What does Wahn want with you?" she asked.

Loki frowned. "Wahn?"

She jerked her chin in the direction of the bird. "The crow. Wahn. That Trickster brings nothing but trouble. Why is he so interested in you?"

"Who're you?"

"We are the Meamei. My younger sisters found you. They followed your tracks to where you'd crawled to the edge of the billabong. It's not safe there—so close to the water's edge. We brought you here."

"Why isn't the billabong safe?"

"You're vulnerable to *him.*"

"To Wahn?"

"Another hunts us and many others. *He* is far worse than Wahn."

"He hunts you and your sisters?"

"That's why we can't take you with us. We travel swiftly through the day, keeping ahead of him. But you're too weak to join us. You need to be careful wherever there is water. That's his domain."

"Why chase Wahn away if he's not hunting you?"

"Wherever Wahn is, there is trouble," the youngest of the Meamie said.

The eldest Meamei sitting in front of Loki met his eyes. "So why does Wahn follow you?"

"He's my protector apparently," Loki said, puzzled at the amused expressions passed between the Meamei.

The youngest sister grinned. "That's unfortunate for you."

"Apparently." Loki gestured to the shelter under the trees. "Were you going to leave me there, then?"

"If Wahn is your protector, he'll watch over you."

The Meamei moved in unison again, their forms flowing around Loki. And as if the seven sisters shared one mind and will, they helped Loki to the safety of the shelter. The sun was blistering hot beyond the shade, and Loki squinted up at the sky. Clouds were gathering on the horizon, and tension building in the atmosphere as if the desert waited in anticipation.

"We'll lead *him* away from here," the eldest of the Meamei said. "If Wahn is your protector, hopefully he'll take human form once we're gone. He's not much use to you as a bird."

Loki glanced at the crow perched in a nearby tree. "I'm sure he'll be useful."

The sisters returned to their conversation again, and the quiet murmurs around Loki became a soothing sound. Dozing in the heat, he imagined their voices as the wind through the trees of Asgard.

***

Loki startled awake to the twilight. Safely ensconced in the shelter, he'd slept deeply all afternoon but now rejuvenated, his usual energy regained. He looked around the shadowy scrub, but the Meamei had gone.

The desert was an endless expanse of subtly changing hues of sand, interrupted sporadically by rocky outcrops and the same slender, white-barked trees as the one Loki rested beneath. From his vantage point, Loki could see the dead river systems where water once flowed from a towering mountain ridge in the distance, across the desert and into a series of hollows. The billabong where the Meamei had first found him was one of many. Even in the gloom of twilight, Loki could see the scattered brilliant colours of wildflowers blooming across the desert. There was such vibrancy in contrast to the desert sands. A Country that was both harsh and pulsing with life.

Yawning, Loki closed his eyes again, head resting on his folded arms. He slept for what might have been moments or could have been much more. A cool breeze brushed his face and startled awake again. The sound of wing beats faded into silence. Wahn had returned.

Still tired, Loki curled up in a more comfortable position. Behind him on one of the large rocky boulders, Loki heard the unmistakable sounds of someone shifting their weight, uncomfortable but settling into a long wait. There was a soft curse, but Loki just smiled and returned to sleep, knowing Wahn kept vigil.

TRUSTING THE MISTRUSTED

Loki woke to the demands of a mortal body. He was parched and his throat was as dry as the desert, as if he'd swallowed its sands while asleep. The need to quench his thirst brought awareness of a more immediate need. His bladder was uncomfortably full from a day asleep. Loki stood and, ignoring the pain of cramped limbs, he stumbled behind the white tree and squatted, reliving himself with a sigh. Rising, he turned to meet the eyes of the man sitting on the rock ledge above him.

"I hope that was amusing for you." Loki glared at Wahn, annoyed he'd forgotten about him completely.

"You make a very attractive woman."

"You find the sight of someone emptying their bladder attractive?"

"No, not that exactly."

"I won't judge you for your proclivities."

Wahn glared at him but said nothing.

Loki coughed, the dry desert air rasping through his lungs. He needed water.

"Did you see them leave?" he asked.

"Who?"

"The seven sisters who threw rocks at you?"

"The Meamei? They left after you'd fallen asleep, and I've guarded you since. Don't you remember?"

"Only some of it. I thought it was a dream."

Squinting at the faint line of red along the edge of the desert, Loki realised the sun had only recently sunk below the horizon. The earth still pulsed with the heat of the day but dark shadows already spread across the open spaces where wildflowers had blossomed in the daylight. From this vantage point, Loki followed the shadows from the clefts and hollows across the landscape, realizing there were more dry waterways than he'd first noticed.

"Where is the nearest billabong?"

"There is one, the darkest of the hollows, over there in the deepest shadows."

Loki shivered at the description. It didn't sound like a pleasant place. Instead of responding, he looked up at the night sky, trying to gauge the position of the moon. *Will I ever learn to navigate this Country? It is so foreign to me; I've got no bearings.* Loki didn't trust Wahn and didn't like being beholden to him.

Loki looked over his shoulder just as Wahn struck a spark and flames leapt hungrily at his touch. The new light cast their shadows over boulders, his own form elongated and monstrous.

"I'd rather you don't wander off around here. You're an innocent in these parts." Wahn's voice was firm, uncompromising.

"Can't say I've ever been known for my innocence before."

"Not even once? How marvellous."

"I think you're about as innocent as I am."

Wahn leapt dramatically to his feet. He walked towards Loki with unswerving confidence, twirling a sprig of purple wildflowers in one hand. He stopped and offered it to Loki with a flourish. Anticipating a jest, Loki hesitantly took the proffered flowers. Time stretched and the silence grew awkward.

Wahn was tall and muscular. This close, Loki could study the intricate white markings that covered his chest. He was drawn to this man like a loadstone and he didn't understand the magnetism. Standing so uncomfortably close, Loki gazed away from the Crow Trickster. Even in the firelight, Wahn's grin widened with amusement.

"I heard you had an unexpected meeting with Yurlunggul?" he asked.

"It was certainly educational."

"It's foolish to walk uninvited into foreign lands."

"Yes. Yurlunggul was less than impressed."

"Yhi and Anjea hold sway only over their own territory. This is not your Country and we move within a complex web of alliances and grievances."

"Doesn't everyone?"

"I think that's something in particular that we share."

"If Anjea and Yhi don't have authority here, who does?"

"I understand your Odin rules the Nine Worlds? Here, we don't have a single ancestor who controls all others. Baiame is the closest being, but you're unlikely to be of any interest to him. No. Yhi holds her own power, but there are many territories behind veils on Country."

"Take me to your lands, then. Surely those would be safe?"

"I don't have any territory. But they *have* left you in my care."

"Leave me with the mortals, then. I'm yet to see any signs of men and women here, but surely a giant snake like Yurlunggul wouldn't notice me. At least until we can orchestrate my escape from Country. It's clear I'm not to tolerated."

"We occupy a space and time separate from the mortal world. While Yurlunggul is a powerful being, he isn't the only one here."

"That doesn't comfort me."

Wahn turned and folded his long legs to drop cross-legged before the fire. He patted the ground beside him invitingly. "Sit with me. Speak to me. I have much to tell you."

The flickering firelight sent shadows dancing on the cliff behind them, and Loki hesitated. Against the absolute darkness of the desert where anything might lie in wait for Loki, the small campfire was a welcome comfort. Sighing, Loki did as he expected to do, following Wahn's instructions like he was a child.

"What do you want to tell me? I've barely got a handful of words from you before and now you suddenly want to have an entire conversation?"

A mischievous smile played on Wahn's lips, but he was frustratingly silent. Instead, he stared at the embers spiralling into the black night. With a dramatic sigh, Wahn leaned back on his elbows, titling his head back to stare at the starry sky. Scowling, Loki copied Wahn's posture and followed his gaze. Again, the beauty and magnificence of the unfamiliar constellations spanning the dome of the sky hypnotised Loki.

Trickster Kin

"You and I are kin," Wahn said.

"What?"

"I've been speaking truth all this time, you've just not been listening."

"You're certainly *not* my kin."

A grin. "You don't know that."

"I think I'd remember you among the fire giants of Muspellheim. So, what makes you think we are kin?"

"Anjea crafted your physical form but the substance of your spirit, or shade as you call it—the essence of your being—was all contrasts and contradictions. She couldn't decide if your form was originally male or female, which tells me a great deal about you too. I imagine in the Nine Worlds, you shifted physical forms frequently? You used your appearance to achieve your goals. I imagine you also had both male and female lovers? If you were of this Country, Loki, you'd share more in common with me than others. We're both Tricksters and you're probably the closest being I have to a sibling."

Loki stared at Wahn, annoyed and unsure what to say. "I was very particular about my physical form. That's what bound me to Odin and got me into this mess."

"Explain." Wahn cocked his head in a bird-like manner.

"I traded my allegiances with my true kin, fire giants of Muspellheim and bound myself to Odin by envying the beauty and grace of Odin's form. In return to make my body as lithe and quick as my tongue and wit, I would be bound as a brother to him

"Then transformation has always been your gift."

"It's more a curse. If I'd never bound myself to Odin, I'd never have found myself among the Aesir. I've never been accepted there and only tolerated for Odin's sake."

"Calm yourself, Loki."

Loki shook his head and stood, pacing with fists clenched. "I would never be here, never cursed by Freyja, never cast adrift from all I knew and never dependent on you. To name me kin! You don't even know me."

Loki advanced with predatory ease on Wahn: movement fluid and designed to provoke violence.

"That would be unwise, Loki." Wahn straightened in his sitting position but didn't take Loki's bait for a fight. "Don't make me tie you up like a misbehaving dingo whelp."

Angry and unable to calm down, Loki kept moving forward but Wahn refused to be provoked. He shook his head firmly and waited for Loki to decide how this would end.

"I'm not your enemy, Loki. There are many who deserve your rage in the Nine Worlds. If you must vent your rage on something, there are other terrors living deep within this desert. Perhaps, save it for them?"

"I don't have enough power to protect myself from Yurlunggul."

"Very few have that power. He's an ancient being and expects all to obey him. It would never occur to Yurlunggul someone like you might not."

"Yurlunggul was very specific that I leave Country before he grew tired of my presence."

"Yurlunggul is the ancestor for this desert, a guardian of Country. Time is very different for such beings. Right now, I'm more concerned with our immediate threats than a being who thinks of time in terms of eons not days."

"There is only one being who can return my form and power to me. We need to summon Odin and then with him, I can return to the Nine Worlds. Sooner rather than later if we can. I 'd like to avoid Yurlunggul's rainbow coils. I don't have the best history with serpents."

"Yhi and I have already given this some consideration. We think there's a way. If we can forge a bridge between Country and the Nine Worlds in a similar manner as how you reached Country, we can link the two cosmoses for a short time. Do you remember your first moments here?"

"I remember a magnificent beach and a wildfire."

"The beach had always been there but the wildfire was the spark from your presence."

"Are you suggesting I set this land on fire? No wonder I'm not very popular here."

"This is what happens to Tricksters, isn't it?"

"To create a crossing point, are you going to set half this Country on fire?"

"No, no. The fire was your own power manifesting. What is the power Odin controls?"

"He's a tactician, a war god. That won't help you much but he's often associated with storms and the sky. His son Thor is the storm god."

Wahn considered this. "Not far from here, there is another ancient Guardian who has a similar affinity with storms. I could persuade them to aid us."

Loki glanced sideways. "Persuade or provoke?

Aren't they the same thing?" Wahn laughed.

Loki gave a sly grin. "I often think so but many don't share that viewpoint. How dangerous is provoking this Guardian into enacting your plans?"

"Plenty dangerous, but let me worry about that one. Once there is enough energy created from the storm, I'll use the bond shared between you and Odin to open a passage between the Nine Worlds and Country. First, I'll need to find Odin and bring him across to Country with me."

"You plan to go into the Nine Worlds?"

"Odin will need a guide for him to cross the divide Yhi opens."

"Make certain to bring Odin's ravens too. He'll need them."

"Ravens? Is a Crow not enough?"

"You misunderstand. Odin's two ravens are his familiars. They always travel with him. They hold memory and self within their forms. We might need those memories to understand why Freyja cursed me and me cast into Ginnungagap in the first place."

"And we'll need these ravens with Odin when he comes to Country?"

"I need to be certain Odin has all his powers with him. We both need to understand the nature of the threat we face when we return to Asgard."

"You already seem certain who is responsible."

"Oh, I'm certain Freyja betrayed us, but I'm less certain about her reasons. We need to be sure she is the only traitor."

"I'll find Odin and these ravens, too, then."

Loki was silent, tracing his fingertips in nonsensical patterns through the sand. "Explain why you think all Tricksters are kindred."

"We share the same power: an unpredictable energy making us beholden to none and our only allegiance is to ourselves. From what I have heard of your story, the essence of who you are and your role in the Nine Worlds is like mine: as if we share the same fibre of our beings. The bonds created between you and Odin break when you wage war against him at Ragnarök. A cycle that continues to restore balance from order to chaos and back again. Now, without you in the Nine Worlds, what happens to that cycle? Freyja is a warrior, yes? Perhaps she wishes to rule the Nine Worlds instead of Odin?"

"What?" Loki stared. "I didn't think that Freyja might want to rule."

Wahn cocked his head reminiscent of his crow form. "You were so certain she wouldn't?"

"I was until you planted *that* seed of doubt."

"I think it bears consideration for why she might want to separate you from Odin's side."

Wahn stood, dusting the fine sand from his hide clothing, and kicked sand over the fire, dousing it. The clouds blew into Loki's face and he coughed, waving his hand in annoyance.

"What are you doing?" Loki hissed.

"We need to walk."

"Now? It's dark."

"You can walk in the heat of the day if you prefer, but I don't much enjoy it. Traveling by night is safer, providing we're careful."

Loki raised his eyebrows. "Careful of what?"

Wahn looked over his shoulder, grinning. "Careful to avoid the monsters."

"Monsters? There are monsters?"

Wahn's grin widened. "Keep up and I'm sure you'll be fine."

Winged Terrors

Wahn and Loki walked beneath the star-drenched sky. A pale crescent moon illuminated a long spine of cliffs in the distance above the desert.

"What's that place?" Loki pointed at the cliffs in the distance.

"Beyond those cliffs is a plateau. And *that* is our destination."

Loki stared across the desert. His frown deepened as shadows rippled across the surface of the cliffs. He peered more intently at the stone fissures and thought for a moment that he saw large birds roosting there. Even as he watched, there was a restless beating of black wings. Fear shivered up his spine. Menace reached across the desert for him. He realized he'd fallen behind Wahn and with the unsettling sense of unseen eyes on him, Loki hastened his pace to catch up.

"What are those birds on the cliffs?"

"They aren't birds. We'd best keep moving if we've drawn the attention of those creatures."

Loki followed, casting a nervous glance back towards the black shapes unfolding wings from the distant cliffs. Despite the darkness of the night, it was still warm with heat radiating from the sand. Sweat trickled down Loki's back, plastering ringlets to the side of his face. The fine coating of dust acquired during the day, the stickiness was unpleasant in the evening heat. Wahn seemed unaffected by the temperature and humidity which made Loki's otherness to this cosmos worsen. Loki ground his teeth in frustration and kept pace with the Trickster.

"Loki!" Wahn's warning was sharp in the quiet night.

"What?" Loki started and half turned to Wahn in bemusement.

"Did you hear anything I just told you?"

"No," he whispered, ashamed he'd lost himself in his thoughts.

"They're coming for us." Wahn ran a hand through his curly dark hair.

"Who? What's coming after us?"

"I knew you weren't listening to me."

Wahn stopped and pointed back to the cliffs. The winged creatures which had clung to the rock face earlier were gone. The empty rock perches were sinister in the pale moonlight now the dark shapes had deserted them.

"Where are they, then?"

Wahn gestured sharply with his hand for silence. He put a finger to his lips and looked up at the starry sky. Loki followed his gaze to the skyline searching for winged creatures. One creature—silhouetted against the crescent moon—accompanied by the rapid beating of wings. To Loki, the beings resembled enormous bats with their leathery wings bearing them towards Loki and Wahn. There was a predatory grace and menace in the movement of wings and revealed long talons against the illumination of the moon. Above them, one of the creatures uttered an eerie scream that filled the night. The sound was like nothing Loki had heard a living creature make and more like sound of wind shrieking through hollow bone. Wahn dropped his finger away from his lips and gestured for Loki to speak.

"What are they?" Loki asked in a barely audible whisper.

"They're known as Namorroddos."

"How do we escape them?" Loki stared at the wheeling mass of creatures above them.

"They hunt as a colony. Before you ask, we can't outrun them."

"That's not very useful."

"Be warned. If they catch us, those talons and teeth will shred us into pieces."

"Again, not useful and not how I imagined dying."

The winged Namorroddos shrieked again and summoned more from the cliffs. Loki turned to Wahn but there was only night air where the Trickster had been. Ahead of him, Wahn was already running towards a rocky outcrop nearby. *He might have at least told me.* Loki swallowed his fear and sprinted across the desert but he quickly lost sight of Wahn in the gloom. He couldn't match Wahn's longer stride and he slowed, breathing hard. Loki's bare feet were sinking into the fine sand again while he wasn't moving. In the darkness, Loki looked for somewhere safe to hide. A sliver of pale moonlight stretched across the desert between Loki and an uneven outcrop of rock that loomed against the horizon.

In the sky, the Namorroddos dived low over the desert with cries of triumph echoing like the screams of dying animals. Black wings circled in a mass, focused on something beyond Loki's intended safety in the rocky outcrop. Peering into the night, Loki recognised the darting long-limbed form in the desert was Wahn. *Is he trying to draw those horrors away from me?* The Crow Trickster moved nimbly over the sand, twisting and spinning away from raking talons.

Loki surveyed the rocky tower he needed to reach. The red rocky structure was squat and widened upward with the plateaued top exposed to the sky. Along the narrow cleft in the cliff there was a faint passageway or steps leading to a shelter. *I have to get there. I can't stand out here, waiting for those winged terrors to feast on me.*

Loki ran for the safety of the rock s. Cold sweat ran down his body and—chest heaving—he ignored the terror coursing through his veins. He lacked Wahn's confidence in the open the expanse of the desert and lacked any ability to outmanoeuvre the Namorroddos. He kept a straight course for the cleft in the rock. He might be a Trickster in the Nine Worlds, but here on Country, the talons of the Namorroddos could pluck him from the earth and tear him into shreds of meat.

The massive wing beats followed Loki and the voices of the Namorroddos screeched with hunger through their bony throats as talons reached for him. He slipped into the rock fissure, watching the rippling shadows move across the sand still hunting for him. From where Loki was positioned, he couldn't see Wahn anymore and hoped he too had evaded the creatures. Even from where he hid, the thick mass of circling Namorroddos in the night sky almost obscured the moonlight and their voices were a shrieking cacophony over the desert.

From the gloom of the sandy expanse, a shadow darted towards Loki. Wahn sprinted from the darkness pursued by grasping talons and shrill cries of the airborne hunters. Loki barely had time to move but pressed himself flat against the rock face as Wahn slid into the narrow space beside him. Into the crevice came slashing talons desperate to catch him. Wahn grinned wildly in the darkness and the whiteness of his teeth reminded Loki uncomfortably of a grinning skull against the blackness. All bravado had fled him and he stared at Wahn in amazement.

"That was insane," Loki said.

Wahn grinned again, too breathless to speak but pushed past Loki and scrambled up the cliff using natural hand and footholds in the rock surface. Still shaking with adrenaline and fear, Loki followed, climbing up through the narrow space. When he reached the top of the cliff, Wahn had dropped into a crouch beneath a wedge-shaped overhang. Here they could hide in the depths of the cavern where fallen boulders had created a natural shelter.

Loki stepped closer to the edge of the overhang and glanced up at the sky. The cries of the Namorroddos still echoed through the night but there was no sight of the hunters. He withdrew back to the safety and sat beside Wahn. If he closed his eyes and listened carefully, he could hear the faint wingbeats of the Namorroddos as they drifted further away to find easier prey.

"What are the Namorroddos?" Loki asked.

"They're hunters, creatures from those northern cliffs. You'll not only find them there but many also dwell in the overhangs of cliffs elsewhere. Few in Country have the power to fight them off. I'm not as powerful as Yhi, but I have learned many skills to avoid beings like the Namorroddos. They've taken to the wing tonight. We're safest waiting in this shelter until morning when they must return to their dark abodes."

"Are we safe up here? Wouldn't being below the surface of the ground where the Namorroddos can't reach us be safer? I feel like I'm just waiting to be plucked up from this rock like a chick in its nest."

Wahn gazed down at the narrow cave mouths dotting the desert hills. He shook his head vehemently. "Underground is home to many beings, and some are worse than the Namorroddos. I'd prefer we take our chances up here where we can at least flee if we must."

"I'll just cower under this overhang then, shall I?"

"If you'd prefer to stand out there in the open and attract their attention, I won't stop you. I'll not be joining you either."

"So we just wait?"

"Curb your impatience and just stay here until dawn. The Namorroddos can't fly during the daylight and they'll return to their dwellings before first light."

"Dawn's a while away yet."

Wahn nodded and cast a quick glance up at the sky. "It is. If the Namorroddos quieten down, we might even get some sleep."

Loki muttered his discontent inaudibly and huddled further into a rock cleft. He wrapped his arms around his knees and cursing the Norns again, tried to ignore the death song of the Namorroddos as they flew across the sky. The relentless noise became a morbid lullaby and Loki finally slipped into a restless sleep.

Planning Chaos

Loki jolted awake at sunrise, his body jerking with the sudden recall of the Namorroddos. Wahn was still sitting beside him and he gently gripped his shoulder, the touch firm and reassuring. First light was brushing the eastern horizon and the sky was fortuitously free of the nightly terrors.

"Where did they go?"

"They returned to their lairs just a moment ago. I think the sudden silence woke you."

Loki grimaced. "They screeched all night? Norns, it is peaceful now then, isn't it?"

Wahn nodded and stretched lazily, but didn't move from the rock shelter. Loki inhaled deeply of the cool morning air and stretched his cramped limbs. Light spread across the waking desert, but Loki still cautiously scanned the sky before stepping out from beneath the overhang. Wahn grinned and gestured rudely at Loki. A mischievous smile played on his lips as Loki returned a gesture of his own making the other Trickster laugh. Loki exhaled and stood under the open sky. *I survived the night. I wasn't ripped apart by talons. Things might just be looking positive for us.*

Wahn still watched Loki with a curiosity shared by crows and ravens. Loki edged further onto the open plateau and, turning a circle on his heel in the pale morning sky, he smiled with lips quirked. A similar smile reflected on Wahn's face and the shared a mischievous expressions made Loki really feel for once the kinship Wahn insisted they shared. There were crinkles at the edge of Wahn's eyes formed more from smiling and laughing than from anger. In that moment, Loki saw a mirrored expression of his own utterly infuriating one. Irrationally annoyed that Wahn was clearly right about their shared kinship, Loki scowled.

"Don't scrunch up your pretty face," Wahn yelled in amusement, slapping his thigh as he laughed.

"I'm beginning to understand why two Tricksters should never be in the same cosmos."

"And so you believe me now?"

"I think the very fabric of time would unwind. We're too similar and the power within you is reaching for that same force in me. It's like two fires meeting. They would consume each other and become one, unquenchable power. There would be a terrible imbalance for me to stay here. My presence *does* threaten the very stability of Country."

Wahn nodded. "In your Nine Worlds there is only one Trickster, but in my Country, there are several, although we rarely cross tracks. I think in another cosmos there could be many more Tricksters who dwell alongside each other. But I can only be certain that your presence here is more than my Country can abide. You don't belong alongside me."

"Do you think there's a cosmos where our kind only exist and there is nothing else? I don't think so. Our purpose is to be the chaos that balances the order. We move between the two forces, constantly back and forth so our cosmoses can be in equilibrium."

"I find little fellowship with the other tricksters of this Country. I've never felt such kinship as with you, Loki. We're pulled to each other because we're the same."

"So each Trickster is different according to their place in the cosmos. You and I share the same role, that's why I create such instability here. But imagine if all the Tricksters from every cosmos met in some other place."

"That would be fun, wouldn't it? Or unbound chaos."

"What's life without risk?"

"I do like the way you think."

"I do astound myself sometimes."

Wahn laughed and bent his head to leave the shelter, careful not to knock into any of the jagged pieces of overhang. He walked with Loki to the very edge of the rock plateau and admired the sunrise. Wahn gestured to the distant cliffs where they'd first seen the Namorroddos.

"We need to go over those cliffs to return you to the Nine Worlds which means bringing another being worse than the Namorroddos to drive them off. Before we can do that, I must meet with Yhi to discuss how best to summon Odin to this cosmos."

"I thought it was only a matter of another being aiding us?"

Wahn avoided his gaze. "*Umm.* Yes, and no."

"Which is it?"

"Probably more of the 'no.' The one who is powerful enough to summon a storm is unlikely to be controllable. If Yhi can create the passage between the two cosmoses and ensure Odin crosses, then we might be safe. These are preparations Yhi needs to make and my plan she needs to agree with."

"Neither of you quite know how to do this?"

"It isn't as though we've had reason to do it before. We're not frequently invaded by Tricksters from other cosmoses threatening the very fabric of our own cosmos and existence. No. We've not done this before."

Loki pinched the bridge of his nose, a headache brewing. "What *is* the plan, then?"

"We'll meet with Yhi later today. She will seek guidance and permission to cross this stretch of desert and up into the cliffs."

Loki paled. "Is this territory we now cross no longer under Yurlunggul's dominion?"

"Yes, and no."

Loki threw his hands into the air, frustrated. "That's not a straight answer, Wahn. I don't want Yurlunggul to crush me or the Namorroddos to tear me apart."

"That's what I'm doing."

"Meeting with Yhi to determine what to do next? That's action"

"Yes. That's what I've been saying we need to do."

Loki stalked to the cleft in the stone where they'd climbed up during their escape from the Namorroddos.

"Where are you going?" Wahn called.

"Are we meeting Yhi here?"

"No."

"Then let's get going before it gets too hot. Walking across this desert is like stepping on a cooking pan."

Wahn grinned but followed Loki into the narrow cleft in the rock. Loki didn't wait for the other man but was already clambering down the cliff.

"I'm going to fly rather than walk."

"Oh, are you? I lost my power to shape shift when I came here. Can you direct me from above."

Wahn rolled his eyes. "Can a crow fly?"

Loki's feet hit the hard-packed sand at the base of the rocky outcrop. He squinted up at Wahn silhouetted against the bright blue sky. The

Trickster's gaze was to the north where Loki could also just see faint traces of gathering cloud. Loki waited on the edge of the plateau, but Wahn just shook himself, his body transforming effortlessly into avian form. The crow hopped along the rock plateau for a moment and ruffled his feathers. Cocking his head, he peered at Loki and cawed. Rolling his eyes, Loki turned and climbed down the cliff, using the same way they had climbed up during the night. Annoyed, Loki began trekking vaguely northwards, swatting at the black flies swarming around him.

Loki traversed the undulating landscape with muttered curses. The sand was already hot, and his bare feet had scarcely recovered from the night's rock-climbing escapades. Where the desert had looked flat from the top of the plateau, he now knew it was far from that. Stony troughs interspersed steep sections of the dune. Throughout his walk, clumps of spiky plants grew where the earth rose, the hollows being full of deeper, hard pebbles worn smooth by the wind and the passage of time. He kept an eye on Wahn, the crow wheeling overhead and angling to a specific location. Whenever Loki passed the dense clusters of plants, he heard lizards scuttling for shelter.

The hollows of deep sand and pebbles seemed to form some pattern, but Loki could find no sense to it. He hoped Wahn was leading through the sand troughs to a destination. A rustle of movement and a snake twisted along the dune in front of Loki. He stopped, barely breathing, as the reptile tasted the air with a forked tongue and moved in a sideways motion across the sand. Since being in Country, Loki had seen so many snakes. He already had an innate fear of snakes and vipers from memories of torture beneath the earth while his wife caught each poisonous drop in a bowl. Sigyn. She'd always been faithful to him and for no reason he could understand. Perhaps she truly did love him. Or she was driven by the feminine expectations of the Norse cosmos: to be a good wife, mother, and honourable. He certainly wasn't so one of them had to be.

Loki has barely gone a handful of paces—still warily checking for more snakes—when sand rose in clouds directly in his path. In front of him, a huge lizard covered in scaly armour squared itself off in challenge against him. The scales covered its body were like the golden rock ledges around them. *Had it been buried beneath the sand until I nearly stepped on it? Why didn't Wahn warn me? Or has the cursed Trickster led me straight into this trap?*

The lizard regarded Loki, its head half-turned to meet his eyes. A pale tongue flicked between pointed teeth. "You trespass here," it hissed and blinked a scaly eyelid over ultramarine-coloured eyes.

Loki looked up, searching for Wahn. The crow wasn't anywhere to be seen. "I'm afraid I'm new to Country. I am probably on your lands in error."

The lizard moved its spiked legs firmly apart. It was a gesture unmistakably of aggression, preparation for an attack.

"I truly meant no offence to trespass here. Upon whose Country do I find myself?"

The lizard hissed and swung a spiny tail into the air. Loki ducked into a crouch at the sight of the rounded end covered with spiky projections. The lizard blinked slowly at Loki. The tail swung again in agitation.

"Wahn!" Loki screamed to the sky. The lizard was readying for battle and not willing to accept any placations or excuses Loki might offer.

The wind swirled as a large crow descended directly in front of Loki, its wings held slightly apart in challenge to the lizard. Loki—ever the opportunist—wasted no time in stepping further away from the armoured lizard. He hoped Wahn could deal with the reptilian desert warrior on his own.

"We seek an audience with Kendi." Wahn's words were a croak, his voice distorted by the avian form.

The lizard hesitated and lifted its front feet in a frustrated movement. The armoured head tilted to one side and Loki saw the open hollow of its ear. Whoever the being Kendi was that Wahn sought a meeting with, he hoped the crow Trickster was as well favored as he thought he was.

The lizard turned one unblinking eye on Wahn. "You may pass to meet on these lands with Kendi."

Loki exhaled in gratitude and hurried after Wahn, careful not to look back at the scaled lizard. A quick glance, showed Loki that the reptile hadn't moved from the middle of the sandy hollow. The only way to pass was to struggle up through the knee-deep sand of the dune. Wahn flapped his wings slowly to keep aloft but close enough to the ground and easy for Loki to follow. Still panting in the heat and still trembling with fear, Loki hurried after the crow. When they reached the top of the dune, Loki heaved in breaths and stared across the mass of dunes that rose and fell like waves into the distance. Wahn croaked at Loki then soared down the side of the dune. Loki followed as fast as he could until he reached the sandy path again. Wahn skipped ahead on his avian talons but neither trickster looked back at the guardian lizard. Loki, for one, could still feel the unblinking gaze boring into his back and making his shoulder blades itch with discomfort.

The path continued until a few straggly white eucalyptus trees formed a tight circle of shade and shelter. Loki sighed with relief once his pale skin was away from the direct sunlight. Wahn shook his glossy feathers and, where the crow had been, the swirling feathers revealed the dark-skinned man with the intricate white sigils on his chest.

"What was that all about?" Loki finally asked.

"The lizard? They are one of the desert guardians. There are many, you must understand. We are seeking to meet with one of the most ancient among them, their leader and elder, if you can understand the respect that earns such a being."

"I do. Wisdom and age are both qualities that are worthy of great respect. But I thought we were meeting with Yhi? These are not her lands, I understand. These would be those belonging to Kendi?"

"Correct. Yhi will meet with us and then we initiate a meeting with Kendi."

"And will Kendi be pleased to see us? Or should I expect a reception like Yurlunggul"

The crow cocked its head at him before skipping along a few more steps. "I don't think Kendi has ever been pleased to see me. But Yhi's presence will assure us of a meeting."

Loki muttered curses under his breath, imagining inventive ways to set the Trickster Crow on fire. But before Loki could consider throwing rocks at Wahn, he took to the wing again. After only a handful of moments, he soared back to Loki's side. A sense of dread twisted like a knot in his stomach.

"What's happened??"

Wahn didn't respond at first but ruffled his shiny black plumage. The inky feathers swirled upward in a whirlwind and then Wahn stood again in human form. A single crow feather spiralled to the ground but before Loki bent to pick it up, it dissipated like smoke.

"Yhi's waiting for me."

"You don't want me to come too? I have a fairly large stake in the outcome here."

"Yhi only asked for me," he said then met Loki's annoyed glare. "Follow this path and you'll reach a large rocky outcrop at the base of a wide plateau. There's a billabong there. It's a good place to rest, escape the sun. Wait for me there."

"It's safe?"

"As safe as anywhere on Country for tricksters like us."

"That doesn't fill me with confidence," Loki muttered. "What aren't you telling me, Wahn?"

A half-smile brushed his lips. "If I told you, it wouldn't be the same."

Loki groaned. He looked down at his dusty and sweat-stained body. The shade and the billabong would be somewhere to wash away the terrors. Before Wahn could deliver any more riddles, Loki walked away down the sandy track, ignoring the prickling sensation of Wahn's gaze on him. Whatever Yhi and Wahn were planning, they didn't want Loki involved. He could only conclude it was something he'd find objectionable. He kept walking at the same pace but when he thought he was out of Wahn's sight, he cast a glance back over his shoulder. Wahn wasn't following him. Loki offered a silent prayer to the Norns, then turned from the path and headed into the landscape of rocky outcrops, gorges, deep ravines as the earth rose higher towards the cliffs in the distance and the storm beginning on the horizon.

Loki didn't walk far until he came to another rock tower with a plateau just like the one they'd sheltered in from the Namorroddos that night. Now, following the ridgeline, Loki noticed another mound of boulders ahead. These were an odd formation as if a giant had thrown the massive stones haphazardly around. The atmosphere was dense with knowledge and ancient power which Loki was unable to resist. He followed the pull of the tantalizingly familiar magic and walked to the edge of the boulders.

Loki stopped at the sandstone boulders. Voices echoed oddly as words slipped between cracks in the gorge on the other side of the boulders. In the center were a few large shrubs crowding a white-barked tree. Loki moved forward with purpose, ignoring the scuttling lizards until he reached one of the smaller boulders. He hid behind it and waited for a break in the conversation and the echoes to stop calling eerily back and forth through the gorge. Hoping he wouldn't be seen, Loki peered over the top the boulder, searching for the origin of the voices. He immediately recognized Wahn lounging in the billabong with his back against the stone sides and the water lapping lazily at his chest.

"You wanted to talk with me about Loki?"

Yhi sat cross-legged opposite him on the bank. Her hair had golden highlights and shimmered in the sunlight. She looked up and regarded the sky for a moment, then turned her attention back to Wahn.

"We need to return him to his Nine Worlds. You've a plan, I assume? Or you wouldn't have summoned me here."

"I do. It's foolhardy enough that you'll dislike it. Before we discuss that. Tell me what's truly worrying you about Loki?" She met his gaze directly. "You share kinship with him and you both thrive on chaos. You already know what the answer is to that question. You want someone else to confirm it for you."

Wahn's lips curved into a quick smile. "I'm offended by your insinuation that I need your corroboration."

"Chaos and mischief follow in your wake."

He shrugged. "Weren't you concerned two Tricksters could unbalance our cosmos? I know Country already has several Tricksters, but we keep to our own places of influence. I'm fairly convinced the addition of Loki to Country is enough to cause a major imbalance, Yhi."

"Chaos and trouble find Tricksters like dragonflies to water. Loki isn't of this cosmos and is too different to fit within the laws and balance of Country. The longer Loki walks on Country, the worse the negative effects will be."

"Did you hear all that, Loki?" Wahn called.

Loki groaned and emerged from beneath the scrub where he'd been hiding. "I guess that wasn't a very effective hiding place, was it?"

"You didn't try very hard," Yhi said.

"No, I didn't," he said. "Now, Wahn tell me what your dangerous plan is and how Yhi can forge a crossing between this cosmos and my own?"

"For the first stage of the plan, we'll need to ask Kendi to sing for us. It will be Kendi's song that puts in motion everything to begin the summer storms. Once it starts, we can't stop it or control the fractious elements of a raging storm. We think Namarrkon will be powerful enough to pierce the barrier between cosmoses."

"And you're sure Kendi and Namarrkon are powerful enough beings for this song to work?"

"I'm sure I mentioned Namarrkon controls the storms? Any, who challenge him by crossing his lands he uses spearheads of lightning to strike them down."

"And you'll be out there in the storm blatantly challenging him? Is that wise?"

"Wahn never does anything wise," Yhi muttered.

She stood and walked into the shadows of the surrounding gorge without another comment to the tricksters. Helplessness raged through Loki and he longed for his power to return, for this impotency to end. Soon, he could take revenge on Freyja for cursing him into this place.

THE STORM SUMMONER

Wahn and Loki waited until sunset—the warmth of the day receding beneath the cool touch of twilight—then stood and prepared for the night's task.

"Yhi's not coming back, is she?" Loki asked as Wahn stretched.

"No. Let's go meet with Kendi. Hopefully he remembers me fondly."

"Is there are chance he might not?"

Wahn only shrugged and gestured toward the edge of the billabong where they'd sheltered during the heat of the day. Wherever they existed, Tricksters were regarded with mistrust. Why should Wahn be any different?

Loki moved from the edge of the billabong but was reluctant to leave the water, its soothing effects and the safety it had accorded. On Country, water was the most precious gift and often hard to find.

"When you flew down to challenge that guardian lizard in the sand dunes, I felt the power radiate from you. You're not as inconsiderable a force here as you imply, are you?"

Wahn grunted and gestured to a large boulder in their path.

"Are you going to answer me?"

"I have as much power as you possessed in the Nine Worlds. And much like you, I'm not particularly well-liked by either the ancestral beings or any of the lesser beings. But I am a force in my own right. Tricksters are a necessary balance in any cosmos as you know and again, it's something we share."

"I wouldn't imagine anyone in the Nine Worlds considers me necessary."

"That's certainly not true or Freyja wouldn't have cursed you into the void. You are the hinge in the Nine Worlds that rebalances everything. They may not like you, but you're necessary to them."

Wahn stopped and held his hand out. Frowning, Loki took it as Wahn began to navigate a narrow channel of uneven rock where sharp ridges and pebbles were treacherous beneath Loki's bare feet. They traversed the rock face carefully with Wahn taking a few stops to gaze across the desert below to gauge their progress.

When they reached the other side of the ravine, Wahn dropped Loki's hand. They faced a smooth stone surface where the rock was a much darker red. Even in the light afforded by the moon, Loki could see grooves and depressions engraved on its surface. Curious at what they might mean, he traced them with his eyes noticing the engravings created in a large concentric circle, the lines spiralling inward until they circled a deep billabong in the centre.

The billabong where Wahn and Loki had spent the day was clearly not the only one in the rising rocky landscape. This billabong, unlike the other, was larger and centered directly in the middle of the flat stone surface plateau and exposed to the night sky above. There would be no trees or scrub to provide shelter from the harsh daylight. Around the perimeter of the stone plateau, Loki saw the familiar white-limbed trees lining the edges. The stark paleness of those trees was beautiful against the blackness of the night. The moon was nearly half-full and the trees shone like bone pillars. Loki committed the scene to memory. This was something too magical to forget.

The power of the place thrummed through the earth and hung in the air. The atmosphere was tense with potential and it reminded Loki a lot of the spring the Norns nurtured at the roots of Yggdrasil. There was reverence here—a place that nourished this Country. Loki left Wahn where he was standing and walked to the edge of the billabong, drawn by the power and pulled closer and closer like a fish hooked on a line. He dropped to his knees at the water's edge, and cupped his hand. Eyes half-closed with a prayer to the Norns and the guardians of Country, he scooped a mouthful of the cool water. Even as the water passed his lips— delicious, cool and faintly metallic—the compulsion to drink more grew.

Wahn had followed him to the billabong and squatted briefly at the edge to take a single mouthful. He watched Loki cautiously before his shoulders relaxed, the tension unrolling through his body like loosening a cape. Loki lifted another handful of water to his lips but before he could drink another, Wahn's long fingers wrapped about his slender wrist. The Trickster gripped him firmly.

"Stop now. That is enough."

Loki's awareness of the deep-sated relaxation flooding his veins came a little too late. The water wasn't just nourishing to Country, there was real power in it and something *medicinal that now caused the stars to spin and the ground to lurch unsteadily beneath him*. Felled by the strength of the water's power, Loki fell backwards and lay still, staring at unfamiliar constellations cast against the ebony dome of the night sky. The anxiety that had been his constant companion since he woke from Yhi's healing beneath the ground had vanished. In those handfuls of this water, he was calm and not afraid.

Wahn watched him with an amused smile. He straightened and looked around the rock walls of the canyon. Unseen beings watched them and with Loki overcome by the water's sedative effects, Wahn noticed the silence around them first. The tiny insects and frogs which had maintained a low but constant chorus in their presence, were now quiet.

Loki shifted to his side, his body feeling like it was made of stone and weighed as much. He watched Wahn's eyes scan the steep walls of the rocky canyon then glance quickly at the open sky above them. Nothing moved. Despite this, Wahn's gaze intensified as he searched the shadows along uneven stone ledges jutting from the cliffs.

From his prone position, Loki stared up at the sky but saw no black wings and couldn't hear the shrieks from hunting Namorroddos. Instead, the silence stretched and became an oppressive weight with the knowledge they weren't alone.

A deliberate movement beyond the white-barked trees caught the attention of both Tricksters. In the darkness, something large moved. Loki peered into the black-and-grey shifting shadows. An enormous bulk detached from the deeper darkness. Loki stood, eyes flicking from Wahn to whatever being lurked in the shadows. On the periphery along the rocky cliff ledges, clawed feet scraped across stone. Loki shivered at the sound, the calm that had filled him earlier evaporating into an icy dread.

Tension roiling through his body, Loki clenched and unclenched his fists. His heart pounded. A lizard, larger than a horse, leapt nimbly from the darkness and moved across the upper ledges of the gorge. Loki stared as it landed lightly on the other side of the billabong. It bared its sharp teeth at Wahn, shaking loose a frill of leathery skin around its neck as though it were the mane of a stallion.

"Crow."

Wahn dipped his head in polite acknowledgement. "Kendi."

"Why bring this stranger among us?"

Wahn ground his teeth but forced himself to relax his arms by his side. Beside him, Loki scanned the rocky ledges and gestured to two slender lizards climbing down from the shadowy depths. Unlike Kendi, these had long snouts with razor-like pointed teeth and the hungry gaze of predators.

Loki shifted uncomfortably. "Wahn?" he asked.

Kendi stared at Wahn. "Crow?" he hissed.

Flinching at the aggressive tone the giant lizard used to reprimand Wahn, Loki took an unconscious step backward and away from them. The unswerving golden gaze of the frilled lizard focused immediately on him. It huffed with impatience, then shook the frill around its neck again.

Wahn laughed, the sound startling in the tense atmosphere. "Perhaps we only stopped to quench our thirst at this billabong?"

Kendi's ruff flared outward again in agitation. "Don't waste my time, Trickster."

Loki glared at Wahn. "What're you doing? I need to return to the Nine Worlds."

Kendi turned his golden eyes on Loki again. "You're a long way from your mountains of fire and ice. You don't belong on this Country."

Wahn held his hands out placatingly. "Yhi and I can return Loki to his cosmos, but we need your aid."

The red-gold ruff fanned outward again, and Kendi snorted. "What do you seek from me, Crow?"

"We only ask you to summon a storm."

Kendi's sharp tongue flicked between pointed teeth. "What you seek is a song."

"You summon storms to nourish Country when necessary. Loki's presence threatens to unbalance our cosmos. Help us remove this threat to Country."

Loki glared at Wahn. "Don't antagonize him."

"Kendi's obligations to Country are greater than his dislike of me. He's more likely to summon a storm if he thinks he's not doing me a favor."

Loki rolled his eyes. "I need a storm."

Wahn stared at him. "Do you ever listen when I talk? Kendi's song summons the storms."

"Then what?"

"I'm not welcome in Kendi's territory. You might've already noticed that. Our friendship is fraught."

Loki rolled my eyes again. "That's an understatement."

While the two were talking, Kendi had leapt up onto the highest of the stone ledges. There was a single boulder that rose above the others, forming an apex.

"What's he doing?" Loki asked.

"He's agreed to sing for you. Which is my signal to take to the wing. Once the storm's summoned, stay here. I'll find you. Another, larger storm is then needed to bridge the cosmoses. My enemy, Namarrkon, is a jealous guardian but has the power we need. We share a mutual dislike of each other."

"How will you gain his help, then?"

"I don't plan to ask him. I plan to provoke him."

"That doesn't sound wise."

"Were your most successful ideas ever wise? I didn't think so. When Kendi sings, a storm is summoned. Namarrkon will travel across his Country, increasing in power as he gathers strength. When he reaches the divide between desert and sea, Yhi will briefly bind our world to yours. In that moment, Odin must be ready to cross."

"Is this dangerous?"

Wahn nodded. Then his form drew inward on itself in a spiral of black feathers. A crow launched into the air and flew north. Loki wondered how Wahn and Yhi intended to splinter the fabric between the Norse cosmos and this world. Could they hold the tenuous connection between worlds long enough for Odin and Loki to cross? Loki had to trust Wahn had partial control of the chaos he was creating, and that he could avoid Namarrkon's wrath. If Wahn was stuck by one of Namarrkon's carefully aimed and fatal lightning spears, Loki could be trapped in this cosmos forever. Above him, the crow cawed, and powerful wing beats carried it north across the night sky.

Singing for a Storm

Wahn's black wings disappeared into the pre-dawn sky. Slowly, Loki turned to the silhouette of the frilled lizard perched above the gorge. The leathery ruff extended around the lizard's upturned face as Kendi began his summoning. It was a quiet song at first, and Loki barely felt its effects, but then the pitch and timbre changed. Loki could feel Kendi's call reverberating through the ground like an earthquake. Kendi threw his mighty chest outward as the bellows of his lungs drew in more air. Loki shivered at the power of it.

The pitch song rose, reverberating through the atmosphere. The strength of it was painful and Loki clasped his hands over his ears. But still Kendi sang, funnelling the raw energy into a final note that hung like electricity in the air, shivering along Loki's skin.

On the northern horizon, storm clouds gathered, blue-black in the predawn light. The cloud mass, heavy with rain, moved infinitely closer, tracking inland as though guided by an unseen hand. The desert stilled around him, silent with anticipation. The clouds moved slowly, lit from within by frequent bursts of lightning. And although morning wasn't far away, the land felt more alive than it ever had. The billabong had a glassy surface, the reflection of the dark clouds above a roiling mass. There wasn't even a ripple or bubble to break its surface. The land waited for the storm with an intensity that made Loki shift uncomfortably, unable to keep still.

A sudden chorus of insects broke the silence. Loki startled so badly he jerked in alarm, nearly slipping into the billabong. The insects sung in a cacophony that steadily gathered rhythm, a thrum drowning out all other noise. Loki shook his head, barely able to think straight for the noise. Kendi's ruff flared, and he drew breath, chest expanding as he sang one last note that soared above the noise, drowning the insects until he met the same pitch. Loki clamped his hands over his ears again, but the noise seemed to invade his mind, vibrating in his skull until he was certain his nose would bleed with the violence of it. Kendi stopped, but the insects continued with the summoning now sung by thousands.

Loki gestured to the desert and its insect choir. "What're they doing?"

Kendi leapt down from the boulders, long claws scraping across the stone. "They're the alyurr. And they are singing."

"But why?"

Kendi tilted his head, amusement in his glittering eyes and pointed teeth. "I've called Namarrkon onto my Country but the alyurr are his kin. They call to him, hoping for a powerful storm, one which will nourish the lands they dwell upon so it can be fertile again."

Loki shrugged. His head ached from the alyurr's song, and he wanted to rest. Finding soft ferns clustered a few paces back from the billabong, he fashioned them into a pillow. Lying back, he watched the storm spiral lazily overhead, circling the desert. Dense cloud cover had already consumed the early morning light. And, against the constant hum of the alyrr and their summoning, Loki's eyelids drooped. Finally, unable to resist sleep any longer, Loki succumbed. His breathing steadied until his heartbeat matched the rhythm of the alyurr's song, carrying him deeper into sleep.

Loki woke as sudden thunder rumbled in the distance. *Where am I?* Disorientated, Loki rolled to his feet, looking around wildly. He was still beside the billabong, the white-limbed trees sheltering him from above. The bed of ferns Loki had been sleeping on now crushed into a Loki-like shape. His gaze flicked to the northern horizon where thunderheads crowded the escarpment, swallowing the last of the daylight. An enormous storm stretched the length of the ridge and hung over the plateau, poised to cross into the desert. Bolts of lightning split purple clouds, brilliant flashes illuminating the sky. Thunder growled, sounding like a predator stalking over the desert.

Kendi raised his scaled head and scented the wind, nostrils flaring. "The one you seek travels on this storm."

"Odin?" Loki asked.

Lifting his face to the sky, he breathed in the storm, hoping for a familiar tang of ice and ozone of the Nine Worlds. A sudden gust of wind slammed against him, knocking Loki backwards a few steps. For a fanciful moment, he was sure he felt Odin's presence. Then another gust of wind struck him, slamming him sideways with such ferocity that Loki stumbled. Cursing the Norns and Freyja with every foul word he could imagine, Loki ran for shelter. He ducked beneath the slender white trees, thinking that this fragile copse was unlikely to provide much safety in the height of any storm.

Rain fell, hesitantly at first, then more frequently. The parched soil greedily absorbing it, soaking the water into crevices and cracks running along its surface. The desert wind rose to meet the storm. Hot, arid gusts blew spirals of red soil and whipped them into towering frenzies. Loki cowered in his shelter as the raw power of the northern storm hit the tempestuous desert winds. Closing his eyes tightly, Loki concentrated on Odin, drawing on the connection they shared. He didn't know how long Yhi could keep the connection open between worlds, but Loki hoped it would be enough for Wahn to find him.

The desert winds turned in a tight circle, swirling dust and abrasive grit against Loki's skin. His unkempt hair was a writhing mass of ringlets around his head. Forcing his mind to focus only on Odin, Loki recalled the scent of ozone, ice, and iron, the sound of battlefields and chanting warriors. This was the essence of the All-Father. The storm intensified, lightning flashing around Loki so chaotically that he finally understood Wahn's fear about Namarrkon. This storm was full of fury and the wildest powers.

A blinding streak of light to Loki's right caught him unaware. The earth rocked beneath his feet, and he fell, searing pain rushing through his body. Raw force ricocheted upward from the earth, arching through Loki's body, and tossing him into the air. He tumbled, weightless and frail as beneath him the earth scorched and splintered, the rock rent apart by a terrible force. Loki burned with agony as he fell through the rain and hissing wind. Two dark shapes like tattered shadows spiralled around him, their forms cutting through the storm like axe-blades. The tempest growled, hands of twisting wind buffeting him, fingers of lightning raking through the sky. The shadows dove and wheeled, avoiding the storm as Loki plummeted back to the ground and the ruins of a smouldering tree.

Loki hit the earth hard; air pushed painfully from his lungs. Dazed, he kept his eyes squeezed shut, unsure if he could even open them. *Am I still alive? Can I move?* Taking a painful breath, Loki opened his eyes. He half expected to see Wahn's grinning face staring down at him. Instead, there was nothing and no one. His body ached as though he'd taken a beating, then broken, and then set on fire by Thor himself. Rain poured down his face, drenching his hair and plastering it to his skin. The soft pelts and the short hide dress were saturated and singed. Loki rolled his head to the side, hissing in pain.

He looked to where he'd been sheltering during the storm. A bolt of lightning had struck one of the trees. The white tree, split asunder, smouldering coals and charcoal, it hissed in the rain. Even the banks of the billabong were scorched, burnt streaks snaking across the ground to where Loki lay, many paces away. The air crackled with residual electricity and stunk of ozone.

Carefully, Loki tried to move his legs, the muscles spasming, the corded tendons jerking erratically. His heartbeat was impossibly fast, and his body clenched in on itself against the burning ache that pulsated through him. Panting with the pain, Loki hauled himself upright. Sweat poured down his body, and he unclenched his jaw. Still, doubled-over with spasms, Loki limped away from the burnt wreckage of the lightning-struck tree, staggering for the stone gorge where Kendi and his kin had probably sheltered.

Limping into the gorge, Loki found it deserted. Kendi and the smaller lizards weren't here. *How did they disappear so quickly?* The storm growled again, lighting flickering across the sky. Loki's heart hammered with fear. *I'm never going to enjoy a storm again.* Pressing his aching body into a rocky cleft, Loki huddled there, fear overwhelming him. An involuntary sob broke from Loki's lips each time Namarrkon sent a series of lightning bolts against the earth. Watching from where he stood, Loki could see through the haze of falling rain that the thirsty and barren lands were quickly turning into a torrent of flooding rivers.

BLIND WITH VENGEANCE

Loki pressed himself against the shallow cleft of the gorge, watching the storm lash into the desert. Lighting strikes sent fresh waves of fear through him, and he flinched with each bolt. Wahn had left him here alone. Even Kendi and his kin had fled Namarrkon's wrath. And now, around him, the ancient rivers of the desert, once dry and cracked, were filling quickly with flood waters, the current fierce. The water was rising fast. If Loki didn't get moving, he'd drown. *Stay here to drown. Leave the shelter, to be struck by lightning.*

"Cursed Norns. Those aren't good choices."

The rain was a torrential downpour, and the storm showed no signs of ending. Sucking in breath and summoning his courage, Loki ran. The red sand that had been soft underfoot turned into cloying mud. And, cursing the Norns, Loki dragged his feet from the mud and stumbled through puddles quickly turning into ponds.

Thunder rolled across the sky and gusts of wind lashed the desert anew. Even the spiny desert bushes huddled together against the wind, their spear-like projections snapping in the gale. As the storm pressed closer, Loki ran faster, knowing there was nothing out here between himself and Namarrkon's wrath.

An electric growl rumbled through the sky, and Loki stopped. *Is there any point running when Namarrkon has found me?* He waited, chest heaving, heart pounding. But no lightning bolt struck him down. Ahead, scarcely visible through the haze of pouring rain, Loki saw a black shape closing in the distance. He heard the welcomed caw of a crow. He'd never been so relieved to see Wahn in his life.

Loki ran after Wahn but slowed his pace. Wahn was Namarrkon's enemy. To Namarrkon, Loki was nothing but a nuisance, but Wahn was different. Namarrkon had a vendetta against Wahn and anyone in the way was collateral. Ran trickled down his face, his hair a sodden tangle. From above, Wahn dove for him, lightning zigzagging across the clouds in pursuit. Loki yelped and leapt sideways. Wahn soared past with inches to spare, the sharp snap of his beak close to Loki's ear.

Wahn continued south, easily remaining beyond the reach of lightning strikes. Wahn continued with his steady wingbeats, drawing Namarrkon's rage and focus from Loki. Certain not to sacrifice Wahn's chance for him to flee, Loki turned and ran for the cliffs and the escarpment to the north.

Running as fast as his mortal body could manage, Loki heard wingbeats behind him. Looking ahead, he still had a long stretch of flooding desert to cross before he'd reach the escarpment. *Why is Wahn following me so soon? He would never make it before Namarrkon caught him.* Glancing over his shoulder, Loki saw two black birds, much larger than Wahn, flying straight at him. He recognised them both at once. He'd know those talons and hooked beaks anywhere. He grinned as Odin's raven familiars, Huginn and Muninn, drew level with him.

Huginn caught an updraught in the storm and flew over Loki's head. As the raven passed above him, Loki ran his fingers through the soft feathers of Huginn's underbelly, ignoring the squawk of protest. Both ravens circled back, beaks snapping at his fingertips, drawing blood. It was enough. Loki felt his blood mingle with Odin's essence, the Sight and Memory that were imbued in Odin's raven familiars. Loki released his memories, letting them flow with his blood, sharing his death at Ragnarök, Freyja's curse, and adrift in Ginnungagap.

Huginn and Muninn beat their wings, laughing into the air, and soared away from him. Rain poured down on the desert. Loki squinted up into the sky. Wahn swooped across the thunderclouds, jagged lightning strikes pursuing him. Loki laughed, watching him. Wahn teased Namarrkon with his airborne manoeuvres, always well ahead of the other being's rage.

Loki was so focused on watching Wahn's reckless antics, he didn't notice Odin walking across the half-flooded desert to his right. He felt, rather than saw Odin approach, a familiar sense of power reaching for him through the rain and fury. A tall figure strode forward, black robes flapping in the gale. Loki smiled to see the simple traveller's robes the man wore as the Wanderer. A name the Midgard mortals gave him when he walked among them. In this guise, he didn't look like a mighty leader of gods.

"Loki," Odin called.

Loki raised a hand in greeting and met the fierce cobalt eye assessing at him. He looked down at his own feminine form, the pale skin, and fiery ringlets. He was nothing like the Trickster from the Nine Worlds. *How does he know it's me? Did he learn that from his ravens?*

"You're a long way from where I left you, Loki."

"Not by my intent."

Odin frowned. "Do you know me?"

"You're an old man in a hat."

"Answer me. I must know if it's you."

Loki sighed, the customary response already on his lips. "You've many names but let me call you by just a few. You're known as All-Father, the Wanderer, and One-Eye. You're Odin of the Aesir. You're also an old man in a hat."

Odin relaxed slightly. "And who are you?"

Loki's lips quirked teasingly. "Don't you remember? I have many names, too, but none of mine are as pleasant. I'm a Liar, Traitor, a child of Muspellheim. I'm also known as Loki Laufeyjarson."

Odin nodded, satisfied, and straightened. He looked around, glancing up at the storm. "The memories you showed me through Huginn and Muninn are how you came to be here?"

"Yes. Freyja cursed me, cast into Ginnungagap. But Anjea summoned me from the void, crafted a new body and brought me here to this cosmos, to this Country. But I am a giant of Muspellheim, and my essence can't be contained within this body. I've had to contain my powers lest they destroy this body, and it made me mortal. I've had no way to summon you here."

Odin half smiled. "As always, you found a way."

"There is another being of this Country not unlike myself. It's with his will and power we've brought you here."

"Another like yourself? How's that possible?"

"Wahn calls himself a Trickster. We have many qualities that only kin can share."

Odin nodded. "I have found you now, my brother."

Loki's lips twisted. "Freyja is not the only practitioner of seidr in the Nine Worlds. Did you know before Ragnarök what would become of me?"

"What would I gain from banishing you, Loki? You're my brother."

"Last we spoke was on a battlefield."

"If you didn't know what Freyja planned, then she hid that knowledge from you."

"I had nothing to do with your banishment. I've been searching for you since Yggdrasil rose from the waters area. Searching throughout the Nine Worlds, following whispered rumours of you. Your place has always been beside me."

"The Aesir have never considered that true."

"Don't you remember the pledge we made?"

Loki sighed. "I pledged to be your brother, and you to me. But the Aesir are your kin, not mine. They tolerate me, enjoy my jests, rely on me to conjure their escape after their mishaps, but also enjoy inflicting cruelty on me."

"My children aren't a threat to you."

"Perhaps not at this moment. But Freyja and her brother are not your kin. Freyja owes no true allegiance to you and yours. She's taken revenge against us both."

"I've been absent from Valhalla too long. We'd best return to the Nine Worlds and see what Freyja has in store for us."

Loki led Odin to the cliffs, the desert red sand now clotted mud adhering to their feet. If Odin had any thoughts on the strangeness of the Country he walked, he didn't mention them. Instead, in the storm's aftermath, they listened to flocks of parrots, colorful birds flying from the shelter of clustered trees around the billabongs which were swollen by floodwater. Loki moved slowly, mortal body aching and burnt from the lightning strike. Flexing his hands, curling, and uncurling his fists, Loki tested the strength of his grip. Ahead, the northern cliffs drew him steadily onward. There was growing dread that their plans might fail.

"Why did you imagine I was complacent in Freyja's actions? Do you have any inkling why she might have cursed you? Banished you into Ginnungagap?"

Loki shook his head slowly. "I've been a cursed fool."

Odin nodded, satisfied. "I think so."

"Not that." He waved his hands impatiently. "Why would Freyja want vengeance on us both? I know you've only got one eye, but don't you see?"

"Not even with any gift of foresight does your rambling make sense, Loki. What're you talking about?"

"Gullveig!"

"I'm familiar with the name. What about her?"

"I told you not to break the Guest-Law of hall and hearth. I warned you there'd be repercussions for your actions. And they're here now."

"Now? But why would Freyja curse and banish you? Surely, she'd target me first?"

"And who, over the eons, has been responsible for getting the Aesir out of every nasty situation? It hasn't been you; it's been me. And when you broke the Guest-Law and killed Gullveig in Valhalla, that was the most unsavory of actions."

"And you think Freyja plans to challenge me now? After all the eons and bonds between us?"

"I think for Freyja, you broke the first law that ever mattered, and she's never forgiven you, Odin. She already takes half the victors from the battlefield, is skilled in seidr and war. What need do the Vanir truly have for the Aesir?"

Odin frowned. "And without you beside me, I couldn't extricate myself from whatever she has planned?"

"How long since you've been in Asgard, Odin? How long after my failure to reappear after Ragnarök did you look for me?"

"Quickly, if you must know."

"And as Freyja knew you would."

They had stopped walking and stood beneath the towering height of the escarpment cliffs. Odin squinted at the storm cell still circling above their heads.

"I fear you're right. How was I so blind to Freyja's vengeance?"

"The Norns appeared as I was dying after Ragnarök. I think they were trying to warn me; in the useless way of unspoken riddles they favour. It did them little good."

"You have a plan to escape this Country now I'm here?"

"I was reliant on you being here. Before I can cross back into the Nine Worlds, I need my powers reunited with my body, but it'll be fatal to this flesh until we've crossed into Asgard again."

"You need my help?"

"As you will need mine once we're back in Asgard."

A Rainbow Crossing

It was sunset and Loki and Odin stopped in stony foothills, making a thin ridge. Wahn had told Loki how these cliffs formed a bluff, and beyond that, a plateau which cut the landscape in half, dividing desert from floodplains. Waiting for twilight, Loki wondered what became of Wahn. *Is he coming back for me? I don't even know where I'm going.* Instead, he stared across the desert Odin and he had traversed. The once arid lands of shifting sands were now swollen waterways, inundated by inland lakes with a single, fast-flowing river sweeping south like a giant serpent. Loki shivered at the memory of Yurlunggul.

Odin scrutinized him. "Cold?"

"Bad memories."

Odin frowned but didn't say anything. He returned his attention to the cliffs behind them. "How do we get to the plateau at the top?"

"Knowing Wahn, he probably expects us to climb it."

Odin raised his grey eyebrows. "Truly?"

"I don't really know what crosses his mind."

Odin chuckled. "He sounds like you."

They did not have to wait long until a familiar black shape swept down from the sky and perched on a ledge behind Loki. There was a shimmer of movement, a flutter of wings and Wahn stood before them. He was naked as usual, the white sigils that covered his body forming their own clothing. A few heartbeats later, Huginn and Muninn flew down and landed on Odin's shoulders. Odin paused, listening to whatever his raven familiars were telling him before turning his attention to Wahn.

"You have been responsible for Loki in this cosmos?"

Wahn grinned. "As much as anyone can be."

Odin laughed. "Truth spoken."

Loki frowned in annoyance. "When you've both finished making jokes at my expense, do we have a plan to get to this plateau?"

Wahn's eyes widened. "You can't climb?"

"We're not scaling these cliffs, surely?"

The crow Trickster shrugged. "Well, you could, but there's a path."

Loki rolled his eyes and turned to Odin. "See what I mean?"

"I like him."

"Of course you do."

Wahn followed the exchange with some amusement and then jumped down from the ledge he had landed on. Strolling past Odin and Loki, he gestured for them to follow him. And without preamble, the leader of the Aesir and Loki fell into step behind Wahn.

The track Wahn followed along the edge of the cliffs was short. Stars were already filling the night sky as daylight retreated, and with the coolness of the storm and the coming night, Loki breathed more easily.

They had not gone far when Wahn gestured to a steep, winding track that led through the cliffs. Sighing, Loki hitched the pelts around his thighs that had once served as modest coverings and were now burnt in patches and tattered beyond repair. If feminine clothing comprised only a section covering the waist and upper thighs, Loki felt certain these pelts were an offence now. Wahn had said nothing, but Loki felt it unlikely he would. He often felt his appraising eyes upon the curves of his body but felt no shame. He was comfortable in this pleasing form.

Despite the steep incline of the track, and the narrow passages where they often had to climb with hands and feet, the last stretch of the path was nearly vertical and close to the top of the cliffs crowned with rocky outcrops. Wahn led them up a section of the track which would have been like steps if not for the vertical slope. Climbing hands over feet, Loki finally stepped out onto the plateau. He stopped, staring at the view that greeted him. So astounded he'd forgotten entirely about Odin behind him. Grumbling, Odin pushed at Loki's feet until he cleared the path.

It was not even midnight, but the three men stood beneath the constellations and stared to the north. A sprawling floodplain stretched

into an endless ocean. Rivers ran like veins across dense grassland and lush vegetation. Even in the night, Loki could see the rivers sparkling in the moonlight, deep patches of complete darkness where gorges intersected the tangled forest. And beyond the glittering floodplains was the silver expanse of the ocean at night.

Odin turned to Wahn. "What's the plan to allow Loki and me to cross back into our cosmos?"

Wahn leaned back against a stone bluff, considering. "We wait for another being, stronger than me or you, to provide the raw power to make such a crossing possible."

Loki ignored Odin's posturing and Wahn's obvious frustration with it, finding a narrow crevice and fresh running water that bubbling up through the stone. *If I've learned anything about Country, it's drink while there's water.* And scooping handfuls into his mouth, he continued to ignore the terse conversation between Odin and Wahn. Clearly, neither man trusted the other, and Loki had no wish to get involved in the contest of pride.

The trio rested as the moon passed its zenith, then slid towards dawn. Then, when the first of the stars vanished from the sky, Wahn stood, motioning for Odin and Loki to do the same.

"It's time," Wahn said.

In the predawn light, the floodplain and its winding rivers were blushed with green. The blue of the swollen river moving to the ocean. Loki remembered the turquoise colour of the ocean when he first arrived on Country amid a sprawling wildfire and thought the pale ocean was probably magnificent in daylight.

Odin looked to the east. "A storm's coming."

Loki's heart hammered at those words. Even though the Norns had no power here, he prayed that this was part of Wahn and Yhi's plan. He dared not imagine what it meant if Namarrkon had found Wahn trespassing on his Country.

"Did you plan this, Wahn?" Loki asked.

"There are a few others to aid us in our crossing. But Odin, I know you're a man who doesn't enjoy depending on others."

"I'm more dependent than you might imagine. My Lady Frigg commands more than my heart."

"The Lady commands Valhalla in his absence. Any who cross Frigg soon find how much power she truly controls," Loki said.

"You'll depend on me and the ancestors of this Country for a little while yet."

Loki glanced at Odin, but he didn't seem perturbed by Wahn's comments. Instead, he'd turned his attention to the two ravens on his shoulders. He spoke briefly to both, then Huginn and Muninn cawed in response, bright eyes glittering with the shared intelligence of familiars.

Wahn led them across the top of the ridge, glancing occasionally up at the sky. Loki followed, lost to thought, heart already racing with the anticipation of confronting Freyja. *Had she acted alone? How deep did her treachery go?* Odin walked at the rear, his footsteps a steady rhythm.

Finally, Wahn stopped, glancing around at the sky and the cliffs before deciding. Whatever Wahn had decided and why, Loki's attention immediately focused on the enormous storm moving across the divide between land and sea, devouring the coastline and swallowing the early morning light in its wake. Beside him, Odin propped one boot against a boulder and turned, brows raised in silent question. Loki only looked away, gesturing vaguely to encompass the storm and the sky.

Billowing dark clouds covered the sky and Loki knew immediately this was no ordinary storm. *Is this Namarrkon's true wrath?* He remembered Wahn's tales of how Namarrkon jealously guarded his Country, not allowing any to cross the divide between desert and floodplains beyond. At the very thought of Namarrkon, dread slipped down Loki's spine, breaking a cold sweat from his skin. He feared Namarrkon every bit as much as Wahn had given him cause to do so.

Loki tried to calm the fear pulsing through him as lightning flickered over the sea. As he kept his gaze fixed on the storm the wind strengthened, blowing his hair into a fiery snarl about his face. Tension filled the atmosphere; the air heavy as though the earth drew breath, waiting and poised for the storm to break. Every fibre of Loki's being screamed with the tension of it; the unspent energy of the storm urging him to move. Agitated, Loki shifted from foot to foot, wanting more than anything to run wild in the chaos.

"Loki." Odin quickly put out a hand to restrain him, holding him firm.

Grinding his teeth, Loki stood, but it took every ounce of his will to obey Odin's command. Wahn, too, was alert, standing taller, his muscles quivering as the storm drew closer still.

Dark clouds crested by thunderheads crossed the coastline. Lightning flickered within the storm, pulling Wahn and Loki taut. Around them, lightning bolts struck the forests and glittered wickedly in reflection across the rivers. Thunder roared in a rumble that shook earth and sky.

"You know what to do?" Wahn asked.

Odin nodded and moved his hands in quick succession, casting a sequence of runes in summoning. Above them, lightning snaked across the sky and the earth shuddered beneath Loki's feet with each resounding thunderclap. Palms slick with perspiration, Loki grabbed for the rock ledge beside him but did not run. Odin turned to Loki and gestured quickly, using the runes that formed their own silent communication. Nodding, Loki squared his shoulders and stood against the buffeting winds of the oncoming storm. Raindrops splattered heavily on the surrounding rocks. Ahead, lightning zigzagged through the clouds, but Loki scarcely noticed. He did not hear Wahn's transformation, only heard the caw of the crow as he took flight into the storm.

Ahead of Loki and Odin, a rainbow shimmer emerged through the storm haze. Bifröst arched into the midst of the storm, and Loki frowned. This was not the usual form the bridge took. Between Asgard and Midgard, it was a spiralling bridge of shifting hues. But here, Bifröst was a solid arch of defined hues, reminding Loki fearfully of Yurlunggul. The dark thunderclouds parted for this tenuous tie between cosmoses. They needed to cross now before that fragile connection broke.

"I need my powers back before we cross!"

Odin nodded, turning his body away from the gusting winds to protect Loki during what would be a terrible demand for his mortal flesh.

Loki turned his focus inward, and crouched close to the ground, knowing if he collapsed, he'd rather be nearer the earth when he did it. Then he forgot the fury of the storm, delving deep within his memories and self. He pushed past the recent memories since arriving on Country, past the chill of Ginnungagap and further still past the icy death in Niflheim and Freyja's curse. There, deep within himself, he found what he was looking for. In the depths of what had been and what he was now, Loki found the lava stone inscribed with the rune for this name. Against the black of the lava stone, the rune shone the fiery red of volcanic depths in Muspellheim. Carefully, he took the stone from where it rested on a flat boulder and held it to his chest. He felt it flare, felt his memory and self return with such force it overwhelmed him.

Gasping, Loki opened his eyes to see Odin staring back at him. He had collapsed, and Odin now held him, sheltered from the raging storm. Loki shuddered, feeling feverish, a surging heat and bitter chill coursing through his body.

"We need to cross now. I have little time in this form."

Odin scooped Loki off the ground and, muttering protests, Loki allowed himself to be supported but refused to be carried.

"I'm not a squalling infant."

Odin glared at him. "No, you're just dying instead."

"Let's just get over Bifröst."

Odin half carried, half dragged Loki onto the solid form of Bifröst, the curved rainbow divisions not as insubstantial as they first appeared. A gust of wind slammed into Odin, knocking him back several steps. Loki stumbled and fell to one knee, staring in horror at the red-and-yellow hues beneath him. What he'd mistaken for colored tracks were snake scales, the shimmering colors exactly like the painted serpents he'd first seen in Yhi's cavern and later Yurlunggul's serpentine coils. *Am I standing on that enormous being? Is this how he makes certain I leave Country?* Before Loki could puzzle the matter any further, Odin looped an arm under his armpits and hauled him to his feet again.

Through the raging storm, they struggled to the peak of the arched bridge. The wind was a furious force against Odin, trying to force him and Loki apart. Clasping his fingers more tightly around Odin's hand, Loki felt him strain to hold keep his grip. Around them, the storm intensified, lightning striking the edges of Bifröst, sending sparks into the clouds. The connection forged between the two cosmoses held.

Sweating profusely, and too weak to stand, Loki turned into the squall. "Let's meet again, Wahn."

Lightheaded and close to collapse, Loki thought he heard a crow's mocking caw in response. Disorientated by the storm, the strength of his true powers destroying the flesh Anjea had crafted for him, Loki held close to Odin as he was led across the divide between cosmoses. Beside them, the black-winged ravens, Muninn and Huginn, called with harsh voices as Odin pressed onwards.

Loki half stumbled beside Odin as they walked down the steep, spiralling slope of Bifröst and descended into Asgard. Again within the Nine Worlds, but still not safe yet, Loki sagged as he turned to face the rift between the cosmoses. Odin raised one hand, casting a quick pattern of runes into the night sky, this time in the reverse that he had used to summon Bifröst.

A blinding flash of light exploded to Loki's right, and he stumbled to his knees. Odin leapt forward, grasping Loki's wrist before he could fall from the edge of Bifröst. Weak beyond measure, Loki swayed in Odin's grasp, head lolling as he stared at the blue-green colours of the Bifröst he knew in the Nine Worlds. *I'm home.*

Behind them, the black sky waited, broken by brilliant bursts of lightning. Wahn's graceful arcs as the Crow kept ahead of the lightning pursuing him. Before the last light of Bifröst failed and the connection between Country and the Nine Worlds was severed, Loki heard the jubilant but mocking caw of a crow. Grinning ruefully, Loki raised a hand in salute to Wahn and leaned his head back against Odin's leg, looking up at his oldest friend and foe.

"I need a form created from the Nine Worlds. Can we get off this accursed bridge?"

An Unexpected Transformation

Odin stood on the ridge overlooking Valhalla. The swirling spiral of Bifröst arched high into the night sky of Asgard before disappearing into the mortal world below. Midgard. Loki always enjoyed the company of the mortal men and women who prayed to the gods, feared the giants, and, most of all, hoped to earn a valiant death and avoid Helheim. He frowned at that thought, wondering how his daughter had fared when he hadn't returned after Ragnarök.

"Does Hel still rule in Helheim?"

Odin startled but recovered quickly before looking down at Loki slumped at his feet. "Yes, she does."

"Not too much has altered then."

But even as Loki ventured the opinion, he looked around Asgard, noticing a few subtle differences. There were always changes after every Ragnarök, things that marked how the Nine Worlds had rebalanced after their rebirth and nestled new among Yggdrasil's branches and roots. Odin scrutinized Asgard, his gaze roaming over the hills and plain of Fólkvangr, and the distant woods of Vanaheim. He focused on the golden peaked roof of Valhalla and pressed his lips into a thin smile. Loki knew it well. Odin's steely displeasure. But the smile softened into a half-grin as he looked down at Loki.

"What?" Loki demanded.

Odin grunted in amusement and jerked his chin at Loki's hands. Frown deepening, Loki turned his hands over in the pale moonlight. He was still female, his body unchanged after crossing Bifröst. He reached up and plucked at the ringlets cascading down his scalp to find they were still the vibrant red of the desert sands of Country.

"Ah, what's happened?"

"I just thought it was very interesting you'd kept the guise given to you in the other cosmos. But your power has returned, I hope?"

Loki ignored the humor in Odin's voice and lifted his hands, willing the fires of Muspellheim to lend him strength. And they did. His body felt instantly lighter, as though he could travel the Nine Worlds with ease. This was one of his gifts, and, he thought, one shared with Wahn. Tricksters were travellers, wanderers without a territory to call their own. If Loki so desired, he might set foot into the stars with nothing but the clothing he wore. *But about that clothing.* Loki was dressed in the tattered pelts that had survived Namarrkon's fury. They were only scraps of hide barely covering his thighs and waist. A thin band of softest hide was wrapped around his chest, serving as only a modest covering for breasts. *I'm going to need something less conspicuous.*

"I'm still a woman?"

"Unless I am very much mistaken, Loki. Yes, you're still a woman."

Loki scrunched up his face in confusion. He hadn't deliberately chosen a form when he crossed into Asgard. He'd assumed he'd be born anew from the essence of the Nine Worlds. And he had been, but he'd kept the semblance of the form Anjea had sculpted from Country. Frustrated at fate taking another twist, Loki kicked at clump a sodden clump of grass with his bare feet. The earth was cold, half-frozen in the night chill.

"Norns curse it," Loki snarled, holding his bruised foot. "I need a pair of boots and some decent clothing."

Odin grinned. "Boots are your greatest concern now?"

"We can't go stalking into Valhalla to confront Freyja and her Valkyries in what little clothing I'm wearing, minus my toes to frostbite."

Absently, Odin scratched at his head and then whistled, drawing the black feathered forms of Muninn and Huginn to his shoulders. He whispered to the raven familiars and glanced once at Loki and then nodded as if a private conversation had concluded. Straightening, Odin waited while the two ravens flew off in different directions.

"Huginn and Muninn have gone in search of clothing and boots for you. If you're certain your powers have returned in their entirety to this form, then I think we can travel to Valhalla this night."

"You make it sound as though this body is unattractive."

Odin glared at him. "You've clearly kept it for some whimsical reason I'll never understand. So, try to focus on something serious for once in your cursed existence. I need a fire giant from Muspellheim at my side tonight to confront Freyja, not a fiery-tongued prankster."

"Although my skills pale compared to Freyja's own, I'm confident mine have returned. This body reflects my nostalgia. I grew accustomed to its shape and quick movements. I'm rather fond of it."

"You're certain then?"

"I'm certain that this is the form I take for now. I've always been a shapeshifter, Odin. This isn't anything new to you. This time, I've shifted human forms."

Odin nodded, seemingly satisfied with the answer. He looked fleetingly to the north where Valhalla glittered in the moonlight, the hills and hollows covered in fresh snowfall. There was a soft caw from above them and Loki whirled, half expecting to see a crow hopping along the snow. But his smile fell as he saw Huginn drop a pair of long, fleece-lined boots nearby, then return to Odin's shoulder. The god convened silently with the raven; the bird fluffing the feathers around his neck in indignation. Another quiet caw behind Loki as Muninn placed a folded tunic and leggings on the snow and shook his plumage, cocked his head at Loki and perched on Odin's other shoulder.

"Thank you, ravens."

Moving swiftly and without preamble, Loki stripped the burnt and sweat-stained pelts from his body, pulling on the wool tunic and leggings, even as he shivered in the cold. There was no belt to tie the tunic, but wherever Odin had directed the ravens, the stack of neatly laundered washing was close to his own size. Next, Loki pulled on the fleece-lined boots, sighing with bliss at the warmth they provided after standing barefoot in the snow.

Loki smiled. "Now we're ready to confront Freyja."

Odin's gaze fixed on the golden hall that was his own. "Let's reclaim Valhalla then."

Not waiting for any response, Odin struck a path to Valhalla, his staff swinging with his long stride. He had earned himself the moniker The Wanderer in many mortal sagas for his gait that traversed Midgard with ease. Following in Odin's wake, Loki thought on the other names he was known by, including War-Bringer. Tonight, as Loki ducked his face against the falling sleet, he thought War-Bringer was the most appropriate of names for Odin as they marched with vengeance in their hearts.

Cold like a Blade

Odin and Loki walked into Valhalla without being challenged. Odin had expected something, a minor skirmish, or even a minor battle, but they met no resistance. It wasn't until Odin pushed on the double doors to Valhalla that they held for the briefest of moments before giving way to his will. Loki shifted uneasily behind Odin as the doors swung inward to reveal the golden hall of Valhalla. It looked exactly as it always had.

The Aesir sat clustered around the two large hearths at either end of the hall, speaking in groups of three or four, some in larger groups of six or eight. Several spits of roasted meat cooked above the fires that ran the length of the hall. Loki focused on the atmosphere of the Aesir, but he followed Odin's gaze to the two high-backed chairs Odin and Frigg had always favoured during their rule. Both were conspicuously absent. There was also quiet in the hall. The constant tones of Bragi's harp were missing.

Loki glanced at the grim set of Odin's face, the thin line of his lips. Blood would spill over this. The Aesir appeared to have accepted Odin and Frigg's departure and continued their activities as if nothing were amiss. It was behaviour Loki had warned Odin about, and he used Hodr to murder his brother to show stubborn Odin the discontent among the Aesir. Odin had not acted then, but now he needed to.

Odin stood in the middle of the open doors, tall and straight with barely contained rage. Beside him, Loki made himself small and slunk into the shadows against one of the oaken doors. Conversation in the hall stuttered and died as the gods turned one by one to stare at Odin. The tension flared through Loki like fire, and the overwhelming desire to break it came to his lips unbidden, all the cutting insults, or foolish jests he could imagine. But he stayed silent. *Tonight is for vengeance, not peace.*

From the shadows at the far end of the hall, Freyja stepped forward. Her eyes narrowed as she studied Odin. She glared and if her gaze had the power of a thousand sword blades behind it, Odin wouldn't have stood a chance. But it didn't, forcing her to contend with Odin. Her lips twisted into a half-smile.

"All-Father," Freyja said, bowing her head slightly. "You've been absent a long time."

Loki could stand waiting in the shadows no longer and let his own power loose. He walked lazily from the other end of the hall, shocked whispers and conversation flowing in his wake. Freyja turned her attention to him, skewering him with a steely glare.

Loki gestured to where Odin's and Frigg's chairs normally resided. "Already moved the furniture out, I see."

Freyja's eyes glittered dangerously, but she didn't challenge him yet. Instead, her gaze slid over him, focusing on Odin. Loki observed her, the machinations playing across her features. She tallied schemes and plans now Odin and Loki had returned. Freyja was no fool, and she had deceived them both to this point. They must both tread carefully lest they get tangled in another of her webs.

Odin stepped closer to Freyja. His sword still sheathed, but his hand lingered near the hilt. "Where's Frigg?"

The shadows behind Freyja shifted as a dozen or more Valkyries, the shield-maidens and collectors of war dead, glared at Odin with open hostility. Loki stepped back to a safer place as, never the warrior himself, he preferred to watch from a vantage point beside a large hearth. Around Valhalla, the gods muttered among themselves, glancing at Odin and the bristling Valkyries. Freyja stepped to the front of her troops, hand closing about the hilt of the blade at her hip. It was the same bone-handled blade she had worn the night Gullveig had burned. Loki realised he'd not seen it at her side for many eons.

Freyja's gaze slid from Odin and pinned Loki with an icy stare. Loki lifted his gaze to meet hers, felt the rage within him kindle into flame. Her lips parted softly as she recognised him. Without warning, she unsheathed her blade, steel ringing through the air as the sword slid free from its scabbard. Odin wasted no time, unsheathing his sword, his long stride taking him closer to Freyja than her Valkyries would have liked.

Standing at the apex of the Valkyries, naked blade held ready, Freyja waited for Odin's next move. But he halted a handful of paces from her, single eye surveying the long hall, resting on those among the gods he had always trusted most. Last, he glanced behind him to where Loki stood by a roasting boar, a small knife cutting a hunk of the meat away. He nodded encouragement and chewed noisily.

Odin's icy gaze fixed on Freyja. "You made an error when you cursed Loki."

She laughed, pure as a bell, but hidden steel behind it. "I cursed Loki?"

"Have you explained to the Aesir and Vanir the reasons for my absence?"

Freyja shook her head, her blonde hair loose about her shoulders in tousled waves. "How could I explain the reasoning of the All-Father?"

"Shall I tell them?"

"I don't know why you've been absent, Odin. All the gods know is you abandoned them and your Lady soon after."

Odin nodded once; his face grim as he turned to Loki. "This is your tale to tell, Loki Laufeyjarson."

Feigning innocence, Loki paused in the act of cutting another hunk of a roast boar for himself. Then, cutting more quickly, skewered the meat on his knife and stepped into the centre of the hall. He felt the eyes of the gods upon him. They had disregarded him as they often did and he'd kept to the shadows in Valhalla, making certain they forgot him as he studied the gods. Whatever lies Freyja had told them, she had gained control of the gods through the vacuum of Odin's absence. What truly concerned Loki was the absence of Frigg. She was a powerful opponent in her own right, but Freyja had seen her leave too. But it was time for the truth, bitter and cold and, with it, vengeance against the witch who had tried to destroy him.

"You know me as Loki Laufeyjarson. You all know the power of my shapeshifting gave birth to Odin's warhorse, Sleipnir, and in seeking retribution for the gods as a hawk, I led the giant lord Thjazi to his death. Transformation is not uncommon among you. Even Lady Freyja has the gift through a hawk-guise cloak. But my powers require no cloaks or spoken charms. That is how I come before you as a woman now."

Quiet laughter echoed around the hall and, although Loki found nothing truly amusing about his chosen form, he knew the mindset of the gods well. Or hoped he did. Freyja *had* deceived him once already.

"This tale began eons ago, before some of you were even among the Aesir. So let us begin, at the beginning. Before the Aesir-Vanir War, before

Odin had the gift of *seidr*, there was a powerful witch. Her name was Gullveig, and her lineage includes many of the völva that live throughout the Nine Worlds, the hated Angrboda and Hel among them. Odin was new as leader of the Aesir, ruler of Asgard, and met with Gullveig and the Vanir. Gullveig had an apprentice, a fierce shield-maiden and warrior named, of course, Freyja.

"When Gullveig wouldn't teach Odin the art of *seidr*, he burned her thrice upon this very hearth and speared her through the heart when she refused to die. But in the throes of death, she spoke the prophecy of Ragnarök. What Odin did that night was break the Guest-Law and strike his enemy down under the pretence of sharing mead and a feast. It is that deception and wrong that Freyja has carried close to her heart all these eons, nourishing it with bitterness and steeling herself for the moment she might take revenge."

Freyja glared venomously at Loki. "This is a fanciful tale. Enough lies."

Freyja rolled her shoulders, blade gripped lightly in her hands, and Odin responded immediately. His sword twirling lazily, firelight shining off the blade as he took another deliberate step forward, testing the response from the ranks of Valkyries. The deadly shield-maidens didn't move from their position but readied themselves in response to his provocation. Impatient in war, Freyja flicked her sword out, slashing idly at Odin.

Immediately, the Valkyries circled Odin, and Freyja stepped into the middle of the circle. Odin's sword kept the Valkyries at arm's length; the tip trained on any who moved within his reach. Carefully, he watched Freyja as she stalked around him, just beyond reach of the sword too. Above, in the rafters of Valhalla, Muninn and Huginn took flight with steady wingbeats, the familiars reporting back what they could see to Odin. The gods stood from their benches and chairs, reaching for weapons, and discarding mead goblets and platters with a clamour of noise. Loki still stood beside the hearth in the unfolding chaos. It'd gone far enough. If Odin wanted to win this argument without a battle, to avoid another Aesir-Vanir war, he needed to stop antagonizing Freyja and start convincing the gods who he claimed owed him allegiance.

Loki sprinted across the hall, heading for his nemesis, Heimdall. The god may have the best hearing and sight in the Nine Worlds, but he wasn't expecting Loki's actions. As Heimdall turned, Loki dove, snatching the horn, the mighty Gjallarhorn, from Heimdall's hip. Sliding across the floor, Loki slammed into the wall and, before Heimdall could catch him, he lifted the horn to his lips and blew.

Silence fell across the skirmish in the middle of Valhalla. Slowly, the gods and Valkyries turned to Loki, who sat on the floor, panting. Heimdall strode over and stood above him, took back his war-horn and kicked Loki in the ribs.

Gasping, Loki climbed to his feet. "I hadn't finished my story."

From somewhere behind the circle of Valkyries, Odin chuckled.

Shakily, Loki walked to the middle of the hall. "Did any among you realize who was absent on the battlefield at Ragnarök? That Freyja never joined the battle despite her Valkyries swelling your ranks? Did none of you notice her brother Freyr sat alone on his golden boar? As I was dying after Ragnarök, the Norns appeared to me. I thought it strange wondering why the weavers of our fates would show themselves as I was dying. I thought it one final, cruel trick. But they vanished, and the trick revealed itself to me as Freyja. She drew upon her power as one of the strongest among the völva, cursing my shade and banishing me from the Nine Worlds.

"But why did Freyja seek vengeance on me? She didn't, of course. Her target was Odin. But there was more than one way to strike at Odin and wrest control of everything he held. Who amongst you has not called me the Sly One? A Liar? But who here has never sought my aid and quick-thinking to evade calamity or extract you from disaster? Odin is your leader, and a skilled tactician, but I have always resolved the more unpalatable issues."

Heimdall stood and glared at Loki. "If what you say is true, why aren't you a shade? If Freyja cursed you and cast you into Ginnungagap, how are you here before us now?"

"Fortunately, Freyja didn't succeed in her attempt to destroy me. Scraps of my shade survived the journey into Ginnungagap and drawn like an arrow to its target, the tatters of my former self found rescue in another cosmos entirely. There, my flesh was newly crafted and my task to reunite myself with Odin began."

Odin stepped forward, staff in one hand, sword in the other. "For once in his existence, Loki speaks the truth. I travelled across the bridge between these cosmoses to reclaim him."

"Better you'd left him there," Heimdall muttered.

Odin twirled his blade slowly and glared at the gods. "And if I had, many of you would be dead by the swords of your brothers or cut down by the Valkyries right now. Do none of you *see* why Loki is among you?"

Freyja glared at Odin. "None of this has any substance. Loki has always admitted he's a liar."

Odin met Freyja's gaze and held it. "How long did you wait once I was gone before taking my place in Valhalla?"

Freyja shifted her sword, still held ready in a defensive posture, but didn't answer Odin.

She glanced at him with malice. "You make it sound as though I outmanoeuvred you. We all know such things can't occur."

"Yet such things are entirely possible if those who intend it are also powerful völva with *seidr* at their command."

"You're a practitioner of *seidr*, too, Odin. I have no advantage over you, no secret knowledge you didn't already possess. I never have."

Loki walked approached the Valkyries, unarmed. "Those eons ago, did you imagine Gullveig was going to win? Did you ever think she'd live with the power she possessed? And do you imagine if you challenge Odin now that he'll allow you and your brother to leave here? The Vanir lost the night he thrice burned Gullveig and pierced her heart. You and I have more in common than you'll ever realize, Freyja. Be wise and concede to him."

Freyja's face was pinched with rage, her blue eyes burning with unspoken hatred. She tensed, bristling with anger. Loki held his breath, praying to the Norns that the weft and warp of their weaving would see Freyja relinquish her desire for revenge tonight. Loki knew that if she raised a sword against Odin now, he'd make certain she and her brother, Freyr, were cut down this very night. Odin had never wanted the Vanir among them, but he'd seen the advantage they brought in prayers from mortals of Midgard.

Odin met Freyja's icy glare. "Do you concede your loss, Freyja? Do you return Asgard and the Nine Worlds to my stewardship?"

Freyja's eyes still burned with rage. She nodded stiffly. A few bitter tears streaked the charcoal applied around her eyes. She sheathed her bone-handled blade and stalked from Valhalla; the Valkyries following like a flock of carrion birds. Loki held his position for a moment, uncertain. Odin turned back to the gods, speaking earnestly and good-heartedly as though nothing had happened. Loki melted back into the shadows where he preferred to be.

Secrets and Lies

The first stars were appearing, shining in the vast expanse of the night sky. Loki stood outside Valhalla; shoulders hunched against the cold. The stars above Asgard seemed foreign to him, like a half-forgotten memory. He remembered the legends and stories mortals had told in Midgard, but he'd been walking beneath another star-map for so long now. *How long have I been gone from the Nine Worlds?* He'd never asked Odin. It seemed irrelevant.

Odin slipped through the double doors to Valhalla, closing them behind him. "You're missing the feast."

Loki nodded, eyes still on the stars. "And what brings you away from the feast and mead?"

"The same thing, I imagine."

Odin puffed on the long pipe dangling from his lips. His face guarded, and Loki couldn't tell what he might be thinking.

"You're not satisfied Freyja has thrown aside her desire for vengeance, either?"

Loki shrugged. "She conceded to you with rage in her heart and eyes. It was done because she must, but no different to when you forced her hand after the Aesir-Vanir War and Gullveig's death. If anything, Odin, her need for revenge will probably grow stronger."

"And you think I should have acted differently? What of your speech to her about Gullveig's death? Those were harsh words for a warrior to hear, especially one poised to fight."

"She needed to hear the truth."

"I spoke truthfully to my kin about the reasons you're regarded so highly among us. It isn't just our bonds as brothers, Loki. Only you can speak freely and without restraint to any in the Nine Worlds. I would have no other ally beside me."

Loki coughed and smiled. "That almost sounds like something Wahn would have said to me."

Odin didn't meet his eyes. "You learned much from that other Trickster."

"You sound displeased, Odin? I learned the value of myself. It's a rare gift; one that's both thorny and precious."

"I am not displeased at all. You've become twice the ally and opponent to me."

"Let's not speak of Ragnarök yet. Let's enjoy these moments where we share brotherhood. I fear what terrors will follow now that Nidhöggr has flown into the north."

Odin's face darkened. "Our lives are cyclic, Loki. Mortals and gods must face the same decay and renewal alike. But I, too, fear the return of the Corpse-Devourer. Nothing good nor fair can come if Nidhöggr leaves the northern mountains."

Loki shivered not from the cold. "You've found Frigg?"

He nodded, pipe to lips again. "She returned to Fensalir when Freyja's suggestions of my betrayal reached her."

"Freyja's suggestions?"

"She claimed I cared more for the giant-kin than the gods."

"That's ludicrous," Loki spluttered than remembered the gods feasting as though nothing had changed. "I warned you once, Odin. Don't become complacent with the Aesir. It allows dissent and dissatisfaction to fester. Once you were absent, those were the fertile fields that allowed Freyja to take your position."

Odin nodded again. "We need to watch her and Freyr. Especially with Nidhöggr in the north. I can't afford to have the gods divided if the Corpse-Devourer flies to Asgard."

Loki bit his lip and cursed the Norns for his foolishness. "Do you imagine your treatment of the Vanir was any different to the giants? You claim kinship with me, welcome Skadi into Asgard and yet you also take up the sword against the giants. When you first met with the Vanir and realised how powerful they were, how much the mortals of Midgard prayed to them, you knew some would only worship the Aesir gods when mortals had need for battle or conquest. The risk you took then is the same one you keep taking, Odin. If I had remained with Wahn, Freyja would have wrested control of the gods from you. You would have lost everything because you failed to see the simplest thing was regarding the Vanir and the giants as equals."

Odin glanced sidewise, lips pursed together. He didn't speak but stood, dark travelling robes billowing around him. "Let's talk on this another day, Loki. Too many bitter words spilt like blood tonight. Come feast with me indoors!"

Loki hesitated, then followed; Odin's hand clapping him on the shoulder. Together they entered the smoky hall. Already the gods had returned to their separate groups, laughing and joking with each other. Beside the hearth, the first tentative notes from Braggi's harp struck the air, and he sang.

Loki let Odin go ahead, hesitating near the wall. He leaned his head back against the wall, crossing his arms over his chest.

Thor approached him, two mead goblets in hand. "You made a skinny man I could've broken in my hands, but you make a fair shield-maiden, Loki Laufeyjarson."

Loki snorted and took the preferred mead. "It's good to be home."

Thor raised a red bushy eyebrow. "Isn't your home in Muspellheim?"

"Are you one of those who believed Freyja's lies, then?"

Thor clapped him on the shoulder, nearly sending him sprawling. "Never, Loki. I'd never betray my father and not my friends. I know more than most how much the gods need you."

"Not just useful for a good joke?"

"You are good at that."

Loki settled back against the wall, listening to Thor and surveying the other gods around the hall. This was what Odin needed him for. His familiars could gather knowledge and be his eyes, but Loki could extract the information Odin needed. And if necessary, set the gods against each other until that information came more readily. Now that Freyja had truly shown her hand, Loki wondered just how many of the gods really supported her, how many just followed the change in leadership in the absence of Odin to challenge it, and whether many felt real opposition to Freyja.

Loki drank and feasted, as Odin had suggested, but remained vigilant around the gods. He kept to the shadows, listening to the conversations around him and for any slip of the tongue that might betray support for Freyja among the gods.

Acknowledgements

There are always many people to thank during the creation, writing and development of a fiction work. I want to acknowledge the long cultural history and caretaking of the First Nations peoples of Australia and their enduring 60,000 years of songlines. I also couldn't have created this work without the magnificent Australian landscape and the lands I walk on shared through my own colonial era immigrant ancestry. The Australia of today is a proud multicultural country and one I draw endless inspiration. Thanks to the team at Brigid's Gate Press for giving voice to *Trickster Tales*, a story of meeting cultures, interweaving tales, sharing stories to share this work with the wider world and my editor Candace Nola for her commitment to making this work shine. Australia is Country. "Always was, always will be".

Leanbh Pearson, 2025.

About the Author

Leanbh Pearson (Any) lives on Ngunnawal Country in Canberra, Australia. An award-winning LGBTQ and disability author of horror and dark fantasy inspired by folklore, fairytales, myth, history and climate. Leanbh's judged numerous awards, an invited panelist and avid book reviewer. Leanbh has been awarded ASA, AHWA and HWA mentorships and 2023 HWA Diversity Grant. Leanbh's alter-ego is an academic in archaeology, evolution and prehistory. A museum devotee, insomniac and photography enthusiast, Leanbh is always aided by canine assistants.

https://linktr.ee/leanbhpearson

DISSONANCE OF BIRD SONG

Alexandra Beaumont

In the storm-riven wilds of ancient Cornwall the sea's whisper will charm us all.

Dissonance of Bird Song is the folkloric-fantasy tale of Eseld, a song-weaver fleeing her home to cure the sacred birds of her people and save her sister. Locked between the lies of land-dwellers and the snare of an ancient sea queen, Eseld must fight to find her own path. Amidst a storm of betrayal and heartbreak, what will Eseld sacrifice to save the ones she loves?

Readers who enjoyed Lucy Hounsom's *Sistersong*, Naomi Novik's *Uprooted*, and Natasha Bowen's *Skin of the Sea* will love *Dissonance of Bird Song*.

THIS COLD NIGHT

Erica Schaef

Following the death of a loved one, Rachelle Collins visits Ferguson Estate, an expansive country mansion which holds many fond memories, and one sinister secret, within its walls. Throughout the course of a single, terrifying night, Rachelle must confront horrors, both psychological and tangible, to prove just how far she is willing to go to keep her family together.

Enter the Darkness

Sarah Budd

During the Spring Solstice, four people enter the caves underneath London.

Garth: a shy young man, who seeks to save the girl of his dreams.

Cassie: a beautiful young woman, who seeks to use the dark magic of the caves for her own purposes.

Bill: an older man with a terrible secret, who seeks to find Garth and Cassie before it's too late.

Sienna: a con artist with a dark past, who seeks to escape her fate as a chosen sacrifice.

Four people enter. Each of them must battle their personal demons before facing the White Lady, who rises each year during the Spring Solstice with a hunger for human flesh.

Only one of them will survive.

THE PRISONERS OF STEWARTVILLE

Shannon Felton

Stewartville. A town living in the shadow of the prisons that drive its economy. Haunted by the ghosts of its past. Cursed by the dark secrets hidden beneath. A town so entwined with the prisons waiting outside the city limits that it's impossible to imagine one without the other, or to ever imagine escaping either.

When a teenage boy digs into the history of the town, he discovers a tunnel system beneath Stewartville, passageways filled with dark secrets. Secrets leading not to freedom, but to unrelenting terror.

Stewartville. Where the convicts aren't the only prisoners.

Visit our website at: www.brigidsgatepress.com